OMNIB

I
CRUDE
SPACE

II
SILVER
SANCTION

III
BRONZE

CRUDE
SPACE

Crude Space
© 2022 Zane Palmer

Crude Space: Silver Sanction
© 2023 Zane Palmer

Crude Space: Bronze
© 2023 Zane Palmer

Crude Space: Omnibus 1
© 2024 Zane Palmer

All rights reserved.

This book or any portion thereof may not be reproduced or used in any manner whatsoever without the express written permission of the publisher except for the use of brief quotations in a book review

TABLE OF CONTENTS

CRUDE SPACE

TERMINOLOGY
INTRO
I PIUS COLONY...3
II Galactic Hyperway..6
Galactic Highway...9
Hadrian Colony...12
III Hadrian Colony..15
Hadrian Colony...20
Hadrian Colony...23
IV Distant Moon..25
V Distant Moon...28
Distant Moon..31
Distant Moon..34
Distant Moon..36
Distant Moon..39
VI Distant Moon..41
Pontoppidan...50
Pontoppidan...52
Pontoppidan...58
Pius Colony..63
VII StarMetro...64

CRUDE SPACE: SILVER SANCTION

- INTRO..72
- VIII Vespasian Colony.........................74
- Pope-I..76
- IX Claudius Colony.............................81
- Vespasian Colony...............................84
- X Claudius Colony..............................87
- Claudius Colony.................................91
- XI Augustus Colony...........................100
- Augustus Colony...............................118
- Augustus Colony...............................120
- XII Augustus Colony..........................125
- Claudius Colony................................130
- XIII Augustus Colony.........................136
- Augustus Colony...............................139
- Claudius Colony................................141

CRUDE SPACE: BRONZE

INTRO	148
XIV Pius Colony	150
XV Claudius Colony	155
Claudius Colony	159
XVI Galactic Port of Pius	165
Claudius Colony	167
Trajan Colony	174
Claudius Colony	178
XVII Claudius Colony	182
Claudius Colony	186
XVIII Claudius Colony	189
XIX Claudius Colony	200
XX Claudius Colony	204
Claudius Colony	207
XXI Augustus Colony	210
Augustus Colony	218

TERMINOLOGY

Crude Space - *Uncharted space in its raw natural state*

Revan-V - *Promethean ship piloted by Code Green from Pro Unit CVII*

WorldPilot - *A powerful psychic capable of manipulating man-made planets.*

StarMetro - *The Galactic hub, one of several man-made planets that roam the galaxy. StarMetro is the unofficial capital of the Hadrian Colony.*

Galactic Time - *Standard 24-hour time frame leftover from the days of the yellow sun.*

Galactic Highway - *A train system that connects the Seven Colonies together. The highway is used to transport resources like food and water, as well as other trading supplies.*

Distant Moon - *An uncharted moon, traveling with an unholy weapon hidden inside.*

Pax Armata - *A peace treaty by force for The Seven Colonies of Man, enforced by Emperor Yujen*

The Nomical Order - *Centuries ago The Seven Colonies of Man joined together in their quest to explore Crude Space and the threat of Astronomicals.*

PRO - *Psychic Response Operative*

PROTO - *Psychic Responses Operative Tactical Officer*

Promethean - *A man-made planet designed for training PROs of the same name.*

Astronomicals - *Space monsters that lurk within Crude Space. These creatures are feared as Gods due to their tremendous size and power. Throughout history, these beings have nearly brought Mankind to the edge of extinction.*

Abysmals - *Alien life that originates within Crude Space. These creatures are unlike anything recorded in the Catalogs of Known Life.*

Catalog of Known Life - *A record of civilized species and organisms that have made contact with mankind.*

Devmetal - *A living metal that feeds on matter and has the capability to terraform a planet. Devmetal is incredibly durable and can be found in most weapons, armor, and even ships. It is classified as an Abysmal in the Catalog of Life. It begins its own life as the embryonic fluid within the egg of an Astronomical.*

the Clear - *Before creation, there was the Clear. An ancient energy source that drives evolution and lives on through the Astronomicals. These godlike aliens feed on the Clear and release the energy back into the universe after death. Over the course of Human history, mankind has developed a chakra pathway for the Clear to enter*

Aurelian Philosophers - *Warrior monks from Aurelius who do not support the current Emperor. They believe one of their own is the rightful heir to Zemula's throne.*

Pope-I - *Promethean ship piloted by PROTO Green from Pro Unit CIV*

Estrella - *Another word for Star, from one of the many languages within the Seven Colonies of Man.*

Werephoenix - *The legendary form of the Uzalech, tied to the solar aliens that rule over them.*

The Sunriza - *(a) Zol and Reya, the last two members of an ancient alien race. (b) A title given to those born with the ability to birth new stars. The Sunriza's people existed thousands of years before humans traversed the galaxy. Their ancient civilization were viewed as gods for their solar abilities. They used their powers to create "suns" for other worlds and lit the way into Crude Space. When humans left their virgin world they conquered star systems from the Sunriza's people. What was once a kingdom spanning one-thousand stars has now been forgotten. The last of the stars under their protection remain hidden within the Nomical Order. Each one feeds radiation back to the Sunrizas, who use that energy to power their techno forces.*

INTRO

Time after time humanity evolves to escape from the expanding reaches of extinction.
The third planet from the yellow sun has long burned out as the human race claims strange new worlds in the galaxy. Seven Colonies of Man, known as *The Nomical Order,* reign supreme. Law is enforced by the Augustus Colony, home to the Capital Planet, Octavian.

The wars that ended mankind's time on their virgin planet echo through generations. There is tension within The Nomical Order. Deep within the Hadrian Colony resides a Planet made from nothing, known as StarMetro. Word spreads of a powerful psychic's prediction, the discovery of an ancient evil. Said to be a weapon to eradicate mankind, in the right hands it could bring about Pax Armata, man's last hope for peace.

Called in at the final hour, an elite team of **Prometheans** (PROs) boards their ship in an effort to maintain order. But even in their elite psychic ranks, imbalance finds itself, as a new recruit joins the unit.

I PIUS COLONY
Revan-V Mid Drift

"Code Black!"
The computer buzzed with noise. The PRO unit sat in rows of two behind their Tactical Officer, Code Red.
"Code Black!"
The machine chimed again. Seated at the back of the cockpit was new recruit Code Black, in fresh attire.
"You just gonna ignore that back there?" Code Yellow called from the seat ahead.
"Code Black!"
The unit shuffled from frustration in their seats as Code Black struggled.
"First time?" Code Green called out. The slim soldier sat behind Code Red and had the largest computer interface. Code Green possessed the ability to manipulate energy. Technology could be controlled with a thought, and so Code Green was Revan-V's pilot.
Code Black chuckled, then replied, "Something like that." The voice modulators in their helmets concealed their voices. Each one of the seven members was assigned a different helmet; Red, White, Yellow, Green, Blue, Pink, and Black. That was their identity as PROs or Psychic Response Officers.

"Code Black!"

The cockpit was alive with frustration as Code Green chimed in, "Greenhorn, want me to bypass it?" The pilot's emerald visor reflected back toward Code Black.

Black let out a sigh and placed a finger on the touch display that required confirmation, and called out, "I got it." The cockpit was silent, as Code Black's gloved palms rubbed together. Green turned forward to pilot through the void of space.

"You'd better be worth the jump to Pius," Yellow called out with a laugh.

Pink turned around to face Yellow. "Watch it with the Pius comments," Code Pink demanded. Code Yellow didn't flinch. Each member of the unit was from a different Colony, Code Pink belonged to Pius Colony. There were six other Promethean units in the Galaxy, all trained on the mobile Planet of the same name.

"Better to stop here than travel all the way out to Aurelius just to pick up an amateur," Yellow continued.

"That's enough," Code Red said with a sigh.

Black kept quiet. The seven members of the unit drifted in silence aboard Revan-V while Code Green piloted.

Once the ship docked at the Galactic Port of Pius, the crew were allowed to leave their seats in the cockpit. The Port was one of seven in the galaxy, used for trade and travel within The Nomical Order.

All Seven Ports connected the Galactic Highway outlined by the first Colonizers.

A large crane arm picked up Revan-V and loaded it into a large freight carrier.

Several vessels of similar scale connected together to form the Hyper-Train.

Code Black stood to exit the cockpit and noticed Code Green still behind the monitor.

Code White and Code Blue, who had been quiet throughout the flight, got up and gave a polite nod as they passed Black. The pair walked ahead of Code Black as they made their way to their personal quarters. Code White and Code Blue appeared to enter the same bunks before Code Black was out of sight.

Finally alone, Code Black removed his helmet in the safety of his secured room. It was comfortable attire, but not something he preferred to wear at all times. Code Black reflected on the helmet in his lap as he meditated on the floor. His mind drifted to thoughts of his childhood, his brother, and his secret mission on this team.

II GALACTIC HIGHWAY
Hyper-Train Enroute to Hadrian Colony
Code Blue's Quarters

Code White stood in the corner of Blue's room and meditated in peace while Code Blue ran a bath. Their connection to the Hyper-Train replenished the small craft's resources like fresh water. Code Blue removed a glove to feel the temperature rise with the water level. When it was just right, Code Blue returned to the bed near Code White and began to undress. Code White turned to watch as Blue removed her helmet to reveal her long dark hair, shaved on the sides and back. Her eyes met with her watcher's white visor.

"You're beautiful," Code White mumbled. The White Promethean moved closer to the bed and her. Code Blue's smile crossed her face as she reached out for White's hand, who reached back. Before their hands could touch White's hand dissolved into thin air and faded out of reach. Code White was a unique Promethean with two abilities, dematerialization and Phasing. The first ability meant that White's physical form could disappear and reappear. The second ability allowed Code White to pass through solid objects.

Code Blue's smile faded just as White's hand did as she pulled away. Code White's hand materialized and pulled away as well.

"Why do you have to be so distant?" Code Blue cried out. Her voice was soft and her eyes pierced through Code White's cold demeanor.

"You know why," Code White remarked on her rejection.

Code Blue stood from the bed and removed her armor chest plate and top. Her naked skin was ready for Code White's touch that never came. Instead, her love, Code White, turned around to deliver her rejection in silence.

Code Blue was embarrassed and rushed toward the readied bath. As she walked away she closed the door behind her to cry alone. She longed for Code White to want her in the same way. Code Blue was able to see the history of anything she touched, an idea Code White feared. Blue wanted nothing more than to touch and know her love.

Code White passed through the closed door as Blue wiped away tears.

"Don't cry, my Sapphire," White pleaded from a distance.

"I-I just want to know you," Blue said.

"You do know me," White replied quickly. Blue stared at her concealed partner.

"I don't even know what you look like under that helmet," she groaned.

White paused for a moment then responded, "Does that matter?" Blue shook her head no in response.

"I live by the Promethean Code," White said, "My identity is all I have, I cannot share it. I'm sorry you spoke about yours with me."

Code White's words were cold in Blue's ears.

"Get out, please," Code Blue demanded in a soft voice.

Code White phased through the door again to return to meditation.

GALACTIC HIGHWAY
Hyper-Train inside Hadrian Colony Revan-V Mess Hall

    Code Red sat across from Yellow and Pink as the three of them plugged in for their supplements. An implant in their wrists all citizens possessed connected them to feeding tubes. As a healthy dose of nutrients was pumped into their bodies the three PROs began to discuss Code Black. Code Yellow used telekinesis to pull a galactic map from the wall and onto the table before the three PROs.
    "Code Black is sus," Yellow said.
    Pink laughed and leaned forward to focus on the map.
    "Those Aurelius PROs are strange folks," Pink replied.
    Promethean was home to psychic humans known as Psychic Response Officers or PROs. The planet was man-made, like a handful of other planets. Promethean recruited psychics from across the galaxy dedicated to uphold law and order. The Prometheans operated in seven-man units with one member from each Colony.

Their Promethean helmets were the only public identity they needed beyond their Colony. The alloy forged to make each colored helmet was powerful enough to keep other psychics out.

Code Red disconnected from the wrist nutrients and glanced over the galactic map. Red's ability of illusion brought the map to life in a frenzy of stars and planets above the table.

Pink pointed to a small region in the map and asked, "We're really going to StarMetro?" Code Red nodded in affirmation.

"The General recommended our unit for a special assignment," Red replied. Code Pink and Yellow looked at each other before their attention returned to Red. Promethean's leader, General Gold, commanded all seven units.

"Whatever the mission is, must be serious for Ol' Gold to trust us with it," Yellow said. Code Red laughed. The Tactical Officer was still focused on the map.

"We shouldn't have any issues," Code Red sat back and remarked.

Code Pink removed the empty tube connected at the wrist and replaced it with fresh nutrients. "Tell that to Black," Pink said.

"I'm serious!" Yellow replied, "Code Black is suspicious. I wouldn't doubt it if someone in the Colonies wanted Black on this mission." Red's crossed arms shifted as Yellow continued.

"I mean, a new Code Black gets assigned to our unit as we're taking this mission? That doesn't sit well with me," Yellow said.

Before anyone else could speak, the door to the mess hall slid open and Code Black entered.

The room was silent for several seconds before Black said, "Code Green told me to find you guys. Looks like the Hyper-Train's approaching the Hadrian Port."

The trio seated around the map remained silent. Code Black glanced over his shoulder. He thought about his conversation a moment ago when a panicked Green said to hurry.

"We, uh, need to take our seats," Code Black chuckled.

HADRIAN COLONY
Revan-V
Enroute to StarMetro

Code Green's mind piloted Revan-V through the Hadrian Colony. The small ship flew through the vast void of untraversed planets ready to be bought at auction. StarMetro was another of the man-made planets created within The Nomical Order. The Machine Planet's coordinates changed every galactic hour.

Galactic Time was established during colonization from the remains of mankind's homeworld. Code Green anticipated StarMetro's relocation was minutes away and changed course.

Revan-V had a mind of its own and was aware of Code Green's presence in the mainframe. The ship had a deep bond with Green and saw her as a mother. Despite their bond, Green dreamed of the day she could become a WorldPilot. Planets made from nothing, such as StarMetro or Promethean, relied on these pilots. Their psychic powers were so advanced they could physically move planets. Code Green joined the Prometheans in the hopes of one day rising to the ranks she envied.

"Who's our contact on this one?" Code Pink asked. Pink being the team's telepath would be in charge of all intel and data while on StarMetro.

"You're gonna have mixed feelings 'bout this one," Code Red replied. In the seat ahead of Pink, Code Yellow began to laugh.

"Don't say it," Pink remarked. Code Red nodded yes, while Yellow continued to laugh.

Code Black asked, "Who is it?"

"Don't say it," Code Pink groaned again, while Blue and White obliviously stared out the windows. Code Green interrupted the outburst to notify everyone they'd made contact. The front windows filled with an image as Code Pink cried, "Don't tell me it's-"

"Howdy, Howdy, Space Crowdy," a loud voice carried through the cockpit as Pink sighed. "It is," Pink said, "It's-"

"Topaz Jack here," The character on the monitor exclaimed in an excited manner. Code Black thought it was a joke at first but the excited man in a mask on the monitor continued.

"Which one of you is in charge?" Topaz Jack asked, "Take me to your leader." The enthusiastic man placed one hand on his brow with his head on a swivel. Code Black laughed to himself although Pink managed to hear.

"Hello, Jack," Code Red responded to the theatrics.

"Oh, so it's the CVII Unit that I have the pleasure of working with. That General of yours doesn't tell me nothin'," Topaz Jack said. Code Red nodded in agreement.

"Ya know, back when I trained on Promethean, I would've made the LXIX unit," Topaz Jack laughed.

"Hard to believe how many of you they go through, huh. Anyway, who's your pilot?" Jack asked.

Code Red pointed over with a thumb and said, "That'd be Green." Code Green was still deep inside the ship but able to hear everything outside.

"Aight Green, ya gotta take the ship to the exact location I'm sending ya," Topaz Jack declared. Green didn't respond but the ship chimed in.

"Why can't we land at one of the standard docks?" Code Pink asked. Topaz Jack shifted his head to face Pink.

"Because, Buddy," Topaz Jack replied, "This location has free parking."

III HADRIAN COLONY
StarMetro

    StarMetro was manufactured with the finest conditions in mind. The planet's millions of casinos and auction houses allow anyone to buy anything from a mate to a planet. Cuisine from all of the Seven Colonies is transported via the Hyper-Train. If you can't find something anywhere else in the galaxy, you can always find it on StarMetro.
    Code Green brought the ship down on the rooftop of an old worn-out building. The neon lights of commercial business shined above and below as the PRO team exited their ship. Smaller crafts darted through the air above them as traffic filled the sky. Below the surface were the echoes of machinery that provided the planet's atmosphere. Code Black admired the smokey skyline as they descended the rat-infested streets. It was his first time on StarMetro and his first time away from his home. Black was raised on Promethean with his brother, and never experienced other worlds.
    "Code Black?" Green asked in a low voice that pulled him out of thought.

"What is it?" Code Black asked quietly to match Green's volume. The two of them were at the back of the group headed down a steep staircase.

"Are you up for this?" Code Green asked. Black didn't have time to respond before they reached two large brown doors at the base of the staircase. Code Red looked around at the team of PROs and then knocked on the door. The large brown doors swung open to reveal a bright interior.

In a white room with black curtains, Topaz Jack sat behind a large glass desk. On top of the desk was his helmet which had a crystal-like quality to it. Along with the helmet, there was a large pile of finely ground space herbs and a cloud of smoke around Jack. The man's greasy wild hair hung across his brow, and his stubble had overstayed its welcome on his sharp jaw. Topaz Jack coughed as he exhaled another lungful of smoke into the air before he put his helmet on.

"Come in, come in," Topaz Jack said as he coughed again, clearly choked up by the smoke.

Code Red sat at the only chair in the room and cast an illusion to create chairs for the rest of the PROs. The team sat down on Code Red's tangible thoughts.

"What can you tell us about the mission?" Code Pink asked Topaz Jack.

"What, no hello?" Topaz Jack scoffed.

"Don't even want to smoke some of my private stash?" He continued.

Code Pink looked at Code Red and asked, "Can't I just read his mind?"

Code Red sat firm, and added out loud, "We need it from his mouth. For the record."

Code Green confirmed with a nod, as she recorded the interaction with a small device. Code Pink scoffed again through crossed arms.

"Jack," Code Red said, "Tell us about the mission."

"Right, the precog," Topaz Jack said.

Precognition was a common ability among psychics that allowed the user to see the future. The scope of the ability ranged from person to person, with most only able to see limited glimpses of events.

"He was born several years ago, the bastard child of Emperor Zemula. You guys old enough to remember what life was like before him? No? Well, It's amazing we have Seven Colonies left after him," Topaz Jack took a second to clear his throat. "Now, where was I?"

"The precog, Jack," Code Red said sinceriously.

"Right," Topaz Jack laughed. "The bastard couldn't speak until he was older than kids in education training, so no one knew he was psychic, like us. When he did say his first words he spoke of his birth father's death, and then Emperor Zemula died shortly after. Because of what he said the kid couldn't grow up on Octavian or even in the Augustus Colony. He was hidden with his mother within the Aurelius Colony.

The Aurelian Philosophers sheltered him and his mother, Aurelia, from the new Emperor. The Philosophers believe this boy is the true heir to Zemula's throne. When the other Colonies learned of his existence some too believed it was his birthright. Back in Aurelius though, as the Colonies neared civil war, the kid took a vow of silence, until recently. When he did finally break his silence he said, Distant Moon."
     The PRO team listened to Topaz Jack's history lesson. "The kid spent about two days repeating Distant Moon until he said something else," Jack added.
     "What was it?" Code Blue asked.
     Topaz Jack looked at each of them and then said, "Ancient Evil."
     The team was quiet for a moment before Code Pink asked, "How does that connect, and what's it got to do with us?"
     Topaz Jack paused to plug a cord into his helmet. A second later vapors released from the helmet's exhaust vents as Topaz Jack sighed in relief.
     "We recently discovered a moon in the Hadrian Colony that wasn't there before, and it's moving. The Emperor's Astronomers have been tracking its course back on Octavian. Their reports indicated it would reach Crude Space within forty-eight galactic hours. That was nearly seventeen hours ago. Once it reaches Crude Space we'll have no way of tracking the moon, or you.

The seven of you will find this moon and bring back whatever you unearth, rumored to be a weapon made in the old ways. Lastly, the boy predicted that a team of Prometheans would shape the future. One member of this team holds the fate of Pax Armata in their hands. The General believes you are that team," Topaz Jack declared.
    Code Black swallowed the lump in his throat.
    Jack sat back and spoke again, "Me? I'm not too sure about you guys, but what does Ol' Jack know, right?"

HADRIAN COLONY
Revan-V

"What is Pax Armata?" Code Black asked. Yellow and Pink looked at each other and back at the newbie with them in the mess hall.

"Peace in the Seven Colonies. Brought to you by whoever's holding the largest weapon," Yellow replied.

Pink chimed in and said, "Don't worry about that Reject back there, doesn't know what he's talking about."

Code Black asked, "You mean Topaz Jack?"

Code Pink nodded. "Topaz Jack is a Reject, a Promethean who didn't make the cut. So there's still hope for you after this mission Black," Code Yellow remarked.

Pink laughed, "Topaz Black, I like the sound of that."

Code Black was offended but before he could speak Yellow chimed in.

"Wouldn't be Topaz Black, seeing as they strip your color," Yellow laughed.

"I'm more than the color of my helmet," Black added. The other two Prometheans continued to laugh.

"If you'd like, you can call me AP," Black said.

"Oh yeah? We're using names now?" Yellow asked.

"Is that short for somethin'?" Pink added.
Code Black was about to reply but was cut off by the ship's alarm system.

■■■

"We should have picked out a nice planet for ourselves at the auction houses." Code Blue said. Her helmet was off, and her focus was on a device in her hand that projected images of planets for sale. The images flashed before them as Code Blue scrolled for a planet to settle with Code White.
"You want to abandon the mission?" Code White asked from the corner where the Promethean meditated. The reflections lit White's visor and the orange trim on the Promethean's armor.
"Not abandon, retire," Code Blue replied. "What about this one?" She asked and pointed to a hologram of a planet covered in water with large islands across the surface.
Code White's eyes remained closed inside the helmet, as the PRO replied, "Not that one."
Code Blue raised an eyebrow and asked, "Are you even paying attention to me?"

White remained still in a meditative position. Code Blue leaned forward on her palms and slowly crawled across the bed she sat upon toward White in the corner. Before she could reach her love for a surprise touch White faded away in place. Blue passed through where White had once been.

"No fair," Blue cried out.

White re-materialized on the other side of the room.

"You shouldn't try to get to know me," White remarked.

Code Blue sat back defeated, and asked, "If you love me, how can you let me live in constant pain?"

White's concealed eyes opened to look upon Blue. "Because-" Code White began but was cut off by the ship's alarm system.

HADRIAN COLONY
Revan-V Cockpit

The Promethean team regrouped in the cockpit as the alarm system silenced.

"Strap yourselves in," Code Red ordered, "We've reached the Distant Moon."

Just ahead of Revan-V in the vast space was a large orb with a strange surface texture. Lightning storms blanketed the moon's atmosphere and concealed the foreign terrain below.

"Looks peaceful," Code Yellow commented.

"There's something alive down there," Pink added. Code Red looked back to Pink for confirmation.

"Are you picking up thoughts from this far?" Code Red asked.

Code Pink replied, "Think so, can't tell what it is yet. Could be Abysmals."

"Whatever is down there is the key to uniting the Seven Colonies," Code Red said, "Let's take the ship down easy. We'll establish a base of operations and begin recon once we've evaluated the terrain."

The unit gave a nod of confirmation with Code Red as the ship accelerated toward the moon.

"Code Green, take us down easy!" Code Red commanded.

Code Green looked to their leader, "I'm not doing this, the ship's flying on its own," Green replied. The moon quickly approached filling the ship's display as the alarm system fired on again.

"It's pulling us in," someone cried as the ship's computer systems shut down around them.

They were dead in the air as Revan-V crashed through the moon's atmosphere. Heavy rain pelted the ship as they descended through the strange clouds. Code White sat back and watched the rest of the cockpit brace for impact. White wasn't worried about the crash thanks to the ability to phase through solid objects. Code Blue reached out for White, whose ability could save them both.

As the ship neared impact White's attention shifted. Code Black, who was unexpectedly calm and collected, was the only PRO on the team not seatbelted in. Code White saw this and grew suspicious of Black but it was too late. The wreck threw Code White from the cockpit who landed unharmed in the warm, sticky grasses of the moon. The Promethean sat up but was unable to phase through the tall blades as they danced in the wind. Code White sighed and began the trek toward the crash site to find Blue and the others.

IV DISTANT MOON

In the hours since the crash, Code White had forgotten about Black and the seatbelt. The team survived with minimal injuries but Code Green said the ship Revan-V was in need of rest. Trees on the moon softened the blow for the ship which crashed down near a large body of water. Code Red sent Yellow and Black to gather wood to burn in a fire. Code Pink assisted Green with the ship while Blue looked for White by the water.

"It sure is hot here," Code Blue said as she fanned herself with her hand. Code White stood in front of her as she caught her breath. The rest of the team was out of sight and Code Blue had White alone to herself.

"Did you come out here to get away from me?" Code Blue asked her love. "You're such a ghost, ya know that?" She added.

Code White turned to face Blue, and said, "Not to get away from you, it's them."

Code Blue felt White's words wrap around her and comfort her. "Okay," She said softly, "I get it." Code Blue sat beside Code White and watched the water. "It's beautiful here," Code Blue reflected on the view.

"It's evil," Code White reminded her.

"Why can't you enjoy what's in front of you?" Blue asked. She removed her glove and teased, "I can see this place's history, if it really is evil, I'll know with one touch."

Code White turned to her, and replied, "You should get Red before you do that." Code Blue placed her palm down on the cold pale surface. "Woah," She cried as the moon shook to life.

"What the hell was that?" Code White asked.

The Promethean looked down at Blue and realized she had passed out, slumped over on her side. White grabbed Blue and carried her over the shoulder back toward the ship. As White held an unconscious Blue for the first time, they were attacked.

Alien orbs dotted the skies above the trees around Revan-V.

These creatures were unlike anything in the Catalogs of Known Life in the galaxy. Hundreds of the Abysmal orbs filled the skies as they descended upon the Prometheans. Pink grabbed a discharger and began to fire low-frequency beams at the attackers. The one-handed weapon fired round after round at the Abysmals. Code Red created multiple clone illusions to fight the creatures. Yellow who had made it back to the area with firewood saw the assault. Code Yellow's telekinetic ability launched rocks and branches into the sky. The Yellow Promethean's tactic provided the team on the ground with momentary cover.

Pink continued to shoot orbs from the flock one at a time, as multiple Code Red Clones did the same. Despite their teamwork, the onslaught in the sky eclipsed all their best efforts.

"Over here," Code Black called out from the outskirts of the treeline.

"C'mon, this way!" Black cried out again.

Code Pink looked to Red and Yellow who were distracted by the alien orbs. *Where's Code Green and the ship?* Pink thought. It was hard to see as the orbs filled the sky, despite this, the creatures seemed to be harmless.

"Over here," Pink heard again.

Code Pink pushed through the orbs that floated nearby to reach the trees with Black, who was with Code Blue.

"She's unconscious," Black declared, "White left her with me then took off." Code Pink tried to look back but a wall of orbs blocked them from the other Prometheans.

"We need to find shelter until we can regroup later," Black called out.

Pink nodded and looked down at Blue. "What about her?" Pink asked.

Code Black looked down at Blue, and replied, "You carry her."

V DISTANT MOON
Code Blue

"Wake up," a voice echoed in Code blue's head.

Pink, is that you? Blue thought to herself as she sat up.

The sky was dark and the surface below her was warm. Code Blue looked around in the dark and made out two Prometheans nearby. Pink and Black were asleep as Blue crawled toward them. Blue placed a hand on Pink to wake him.

"Don't touch me," Pink said in a mumbled tone.

"Apax, huh?" Code Blue replied. She had learned about Pink from their contact.

"Ciela, huh?" Pink fired back, "Don't say my name again, and don't touch me, your power works both ways thanks to my telepathy."

Code Blue leaned back away from Pink and asked, "How does that work?"

Code Pink sat up and dusted himself off. "Our helmets block my mind from getting in your head, but if we touch you become an extension of me, allowing me inside."

"That's interesting," Code Blue replied, "How much do you know about Code White?"

Code Pink laughed and shook his head, "Too much after peeking inside your head."

"Okay, forget it," Code Blue said in a soft tone. After a long pause, she asked, "Should we wake up Black now?"

Code Pink nodded and turned his attention to the third Promethean.

Code Blue approached Black asleep on his side but before she could get to him he called out, "I'm awake." Code Black sat up to join the others.

"How long have you been up?" Code Pink questioned.

Black stood up from the ground and laughed, "Somewhere after your formal introductions."

Pink and Blue got to their feet and the three of them surveyed the area. The night sky made it difficult to see, but they could make out a large forest nearby.

"We should avoid going in there," Pink remarked.

"Do you think the others have found anything yet?" Blue asked, her mind still focused on Code White.

"We have now," A voice called out. Blue thought maybe this was the person who woke her earlier. Code Red emerged from the darkness and greeted the three Prometheans.

"Where's everyone else?" Code Pink asked their leader.

Black kept his focus on the dark horizon as thick fog rolled in.

Code Red shrugged, and said, "You're the first I've found. They could be anywhere on this moon after that attack today."

Code Black turned to the other three and commented, "There's a mountain off in the distance to our left. Should we look for the others there?"

DISTANT MOON
Code Yellow

    Code Yellow managed to take shelter in the tall grass that shielded him from the orbs. Hours passed before the Promethean moved. The adhesive grass restricted Yellow, who used telekinesis to cut free. The sky was cloudy and the air was humid. The silhouette of a mountain peeked through the foggy horizon as Code Yellow marched on. The neon sunset faded before the Promethean reached the base of the mountain. The thick fog parted telekinetically around Code Yellow. The low visibility was hardly enough to slow Yellow down in his pursuit of the mission. Code Yellow concentrated inward as his feet and body levitated into the air. It was easy to manipulate other objects, but Yellow struggled to use it on himself this way.
    "Avi," a familiar voice called out. Yellow lost focus and crashed down to the surface with a thud.
    "Argh," Yellow groaned from the impact. The Promethean looked around in the dark.
    "Elma? Where are you?" Yellow called out. The terrain offered lots of places to hide.
    Code Red leaned in and extended a hand to Yellow who accepted.

"C'mon, get up," the Promethean Leader said as Code Yellow stood up off the ground.

"How'd you find me out here?" Yellow asked with mixed emotions about the Unit Leader.

Code Red dusted off her fellow Promethean and looked to the mountain.

"How long have we been doing this, Avi?" Red asked, "I know you've got a greedy side. Did you think you'd go off exploring on your own? Did you plan to find the weapon first?"

Yellow looked to Red, someone he had known as a sister, and remarked, "I'm not the only one out here in the dark alone. Have you sent your illusions out to find the others yet? Or are we climbing this mountain by ourselves?"

Red didn't respond, instead, she turned her attention to the mountain. A bright light emitted from what appeared to be a cave entrance at the top.

"What makes you think this is it?" Red asked, her focus shifted from the mountain back to Code Yellow.

"El, you don't find that suspicious?" Code Yellow replied, his arm extended out toward the glow of the mountain.

Red concentrated her ability for a moment then looked at Yellow and said, "Okay. I just told my illusions where we are, so they know to bring anyone they find to the mountain. No funny business up there, got it?"

"After me," Yellow laughed as he took the lead up the mountain. Code Red smirked under her helmet as she followed close behind.

DISTANT MOON
Code Green
Revan-V

    Code Green worked diligently to repair Revan-V after their unexpected crash. The Promethean pilot could hear the ship's pain in her head as it cried out for its mother.
    "I'm here," Green whispered as she unscrewed the panels to the engine.
    "We're going to get out of here," She reassured the ship.
    It was hard to work in the dark but the emerald Promethean didn't give up on her baby. They were all alone after the attack separated Green and the ship from the team. Green's mission was to get Revan-V stable for takeoff before the moon hit Crude Space. Sparks shot out from inside the engine house and ricocheted off of Green's visor.
    "Is it that bad?" A voice called out from behind Green, who jumped in response. The Green Promethean turned back to see Code Red behind her.
    "Oh, hey," Green replied.
    Code Red looked over Green's shoulder at the engine, and said, "You don't sound happy to see me."
    Green swallowed the lump in her throat.

"It's this ship, ya know," Code Green laughed, unsure how to feel with Red there.

"Well, is there anything I can do to help?" The Red leader asked.

Green sighed, and said, "No, just need some more time."

Green looked at the ship lovingly and added, "This ship's seen worse. We'll be ready to go by the time the others join us. By the way, have you found any of the others yet?"

Red looked in the distance at the mountain in the fog. "Not yet," Red lied.

DISTANT MOON
Code Black

Code Black followed Red, Pink, and Blue while they argued over which direction to travel. Fog lingered around the Prometheans, and thick trees crowded their path.

"This is the way," Code Red commented.

Her crimson helmet shined through the fog as Pink replied, "Really?" Because something's telling me to go to that mountain." Code Pink's muscular arm extended out toward the ominous mountain on the horizon.

Code Blue was distracted by the moon and bumped into Code Pink ahead of her. Code Blue felt Pink's emotions engulf her through their contact. Anger and doubt rushed through Blue as she felt her adrenaline rise to match Code Pink's, but only for a moment.

"Are you questioning your team lead?" Code Red asked. Her arm was extended towards Pink with her index finger stretched out in his face.

Code Pink stood calm and simply shook his head, and declared, "No, Red. But I've seen your pride get in the way before, it's okay if you're lost. And if you say you're leading us to your other selves and to the rest of the team, I'll take your word for it. But there's a voice in my head that's telling me to go to the mountain."

Code Blue perked up when she heard Pink's comment and chimed in, "Do you mean *Pontoppidan*?"

Code Red and Pink turned their attention to Blue as she asked, "Is he speaking to you, too?"

Code Black might as well have been invisible to the three Prometheans, but he remained silent.

"Who are you talking about?" The team leader, Code Red demanded.

Code Blue looked over to Pink, "**Pontoppidan**. He's mad that we're here, he's still sleeping so we don't want to wake him."

Code Black looked around in the fog, but only saw trees and Prometheans.

"Is he at the mountain?" Code Pink asked Blue.

Blue thought about it for a moment but shook her head no, and said, "I don't know where he is, but he's close."

Code Red wanted to take back control of the situation, and the team.

"We can figure this out once the seven of us have regrouped," Red added, "Let's get back on track."

Code Red turned before the team had a chance to respond and marched into the fog.

Code Pink called out behind her, "Red, how about this. You take these two with you to get the others, then everyone meets me at the mountain."

Code Blue shot a glance at Pink, impressed that he had challenged Red's leadership. Black observed his teammates as tension rose among them.

Before Red could respond, Pink added, "Hell, I'll even take one of you with me, just think me up a clone of yourself, and let's go."

"I want to go with Pink," Code Black declared, his hand went into the air as he broke his silence.

Code Blue looked back to Black who was a few feet from the others. She had forgotten the new recruit was with them this whole time.

"Me too," Code Blue spoke softly.

Code Red sighed as she realized she was outnumbered. "If this is what you want," Red said, "I'll tell my other selves to meet us there, But I promise you we're not going to find anything."

DISTANT MOON
Code Green
Revan-V

"How's the ship?" Code Red questioned.

Code Green was on her back under the hull of the craft as she unscrewed thick bolts to the battery house.

"Same as it was five minutes ago," Green called out as she got the last bolt off.

The battery door dropped open inches away from Green's visor. *I'm sorry*, Green's thoughts communicated to the ship. She removed a wire from a pouch on her belt and plugged it into the slot on her wrist. Green inserted the other end into the battery of the ship and winced as energy flooded into her body.

Code Green knew it would be a few minutes before the ship's battery would be completely drained.

"Hey Red," Code Green asked, "Are you worried about the others? Since your copies haven't found anyone else yet?"

Code Red bent down to check on Green below the ship. "Let's just worry about the ship," Code Red replied, as she paused to keep her focus on Green.

"I'm sure the others will find the weapon one way or another," Code Red added.

Code Green doubted Red's words and continued to tinker on the battery until Red stood. Green lowered her arm connected to the battery and sighed.

I hope you guys are okay out there, Green thought as Red slowly walked away from Revan-V.

Code Red's attention shifted to the distant mountain, where the others had gathered.

VI DISTANT MOON
Code Pink

Abysmal orbs descended through the foggy skies as the Prometheans ran.

"They came out of nowhere," Code Blue cried out as she ran behind Red.

The terrain was difficult to navigate as Pink led the group toward the base of the mountain.

"There's a path this way," Pink yelled, as he fired bolts from his discharger into the flock of orbs above.

"These things are persistent," Code Red remarked. The Promethean cast her illusions to form a large shield for cover from the aerial attack.

Code Black caught up to the others as the orbs continued their dance in the sky around the mountain.

"I think we're clear to go up," Code Blue said through tired breaths.

The mouth of a cave above them emitted a strange light.

"Who wants to go first?" Red asked.

The four Prometheans reached the cave with no interference from the orbs. Once inside a large open area ended with a staircase that led into the mountain. "We're going below the surface?" Code Black asked.

"Down here," Pink heard a voice echo from the stairs.

"Did you guys hear that?" Code Pink called out, running toward the stairs.

Code Black was at the rear of the team going down hundreds of polished stairs.

This was man-made, Code Black thought about the structural integrity of the cavern.

"Hurry," The voice echoed again to Pink.

The four of them reached the bottom of the staircase. Two large doors stood before them cracked open.

"Is this Pontoppidan person in there?" Code Black asked Blue quietly.

Blue looked over to her fellow Promethean to give a response but Code Pink began to yell to get inside.

"Where's the fire?" Code Yellow laughed as the Prometheans charged into the chamber behind the doors.

Another Code Red stood beside Yellow at an altar in the center of the room. "What is this?" Code Pink called out.

"He's here," Code Blue cried. The team turned their attention to Blue, who fell to her knees.

"He's here," Code Blue cried again.

Code Yellow was confused and looked at *his* Red and asked, "Do you know what she's talking about?"

The Code Red that was with Yellow nodded and replied, **"Pontoppidan."**

"Where is he?" Code Pink called out, his focus was on Code Yellow and the Red with him at the altar.

"H-He," Code Blue's voice was broken, "**He's awake**," She cried out on all fours.

Code Black's head was on a swivel, but he only saw his fellow Prometheans.

"You're talking about the moon, aren't you? This moon is Pontoppidan?" Code Pink asked Blue, still focused on the others. Code Blue nodded from the ground as she tried to regain her composure.

"What happens if he wakes up?" Code Black asked.

Blue turned and said, "Right now we have less than twenty-four hours until the moon hits Crude Space. If Pontoppidan's drifting through space asleep at this speed, imagine where he could take us if he woke up."

Code Black swallowed a lump in his throat.

"Not to mention his muscles are so massive that if he were to willingly move the force could crush us all," Code Pink added.

Code Black looked at Blue and asked, "How do you know all this?"

Code Pink examined the altar in the room and wondered why it was empty.

"When I was alone with White earlier, I touched the surface and felt its history," Code Blue confessed. *Code White!* Code Blue thought about her love, *I hope you're okay out there.*

"We can't do anything if Pontoppidan is awake, we can only pray he's not aware of us. What is this room?" Code Pink questioned as he surveyed the room.

Code Yellow and Red looked at each other, "Right, the room," Code Red replied.

"We got down here right before you guys showed up," Code Yellow added.

Pink's attention was on the empty altar, "What about that," Code Pink asked as he pointed to the altar.

The two Prometheans laughed together, "What about it?" Red asked.

"Did you find the weapon?" Pink asked, growing frustrated with his fellow Prometheans.

"We didn't find a weapon, but we found this," Yellow said, as a black box levitated from behind his back.

"What is it?" Code Black called out from beside Blue and the Red that traveled with them.

"We didn't want to touch it until you got here Blue," Red confessed, her focus turned to the wooden box between them.

"Yeah, sure, let me take all the risks," Blue said as she approached the others at the altar.

Do not touch that time coffin, A voice echoed in Blue's head.

Pontoppidan? Blue thought in response.

Yes, child, Pontoppidan replied in Blue's head, *That box is evil, a remnant of the past that should not exist.*

Code Blue walked up the steps to the altar in the center of the room to meet Yellow and Red at the box. "What do you want me to do?" Code Blue asked as she removed her glove to reveal her skin.

"Open it," Code Red replied, the Promethean leader at the altar looked over to Yellow.

"Which one of you is the real Red?" Code Pink demanded before Blue could touch the box.

Blue's hand hesitated, as the Red that was at the altar replied, "That doesn't matter, Blue, open the box."

Code Blue turned to Pink and lowered her exposed hand.

"Open the box," Red yelled at Blue as she grabbed her by the wrist and lifted her hand to the box. Code Blue screamed in pain from the contact with Red as her exposed hand was placed on the cold wooden box.

Pink fired his discharger at the Code Red that stood at the altar, but the shot passed through her illusion body. The box cracked open from Blue's touch as she collapsed to the floor.

"What did you do?" Code Black called out in all the confusion.

The ground shook below them as Pontoppidan awoke. The force of energy was enough to bring Blue back to her feet despite being drained seconds before. Orbs flew into the cave as Pontoppidan's muscles shifted. The creature had wrapped his eight long tentacles around his body to protect his head.

"He's been asleep for centuries, and now it'll be centuries before he naps again," Blue commented.

"That'll give me plenty of time to fly this thing back to Octavian," Red laughed.

Red's illusion at the altar gave Code Pink a round of applause.

"That would've been a good shot," Red said with a chuckle. The Promethean leader looked at the opened box on the ground.

Code Pink aimed his discharger at the Red he'd traveled with and yelled, "What did you do Red?"

Code Red shielded herself as the other walked toward the box and reached inside.

"What is going on?" Code Black demanded. He looked to Code Blue for answers since her ability would have filled her in.

Code Pink fired his weapon again, but it passed through this Red as well. "Goddammit, where's the real you?" Pink screamed out.

Code Blue whispered to Black, "When Red touched me I saw what happened."

Code Pink flipped a switch on his discharger to fire lethal rounds. "I know you killed Yellow to get down here," Code Pink confessed. Pink aimed his weapon at Code Yellow, who raised his hands in defense.

"Avi loved you like a sister, El, and you killed him," Pink cried out, "But you made a mistake. You took his helmet before he was dead and his final thoughts led me down here."

Pink fired his discharger at Yellow's helmet in an explosion of sparks. The Promethean fell to the floor as the rest of the team watched. Red's illusions faded away beside the fallen Code Yellow.
    Code Pink went to the box and collected what was inside.
    "Do you realize what this is?" Pink asked, in his hands was a large black egg.
    Blue nodded to Pink who regrouped with her and Code Black.
    "Ancient evil," Blue replied.
    "What is it really?" Code Black asked anxiously.
    "We'll tell you on the way back to the ship," Code Pink said. Code Pink turned to Blue and handed her the egg.
    "What about Red?" Code Blue asked.
    "I'm not carrying a body," Code Black replied.
    "We have what we need," Code Pink added.
    The three made their way up the stairs toward the entrance of the cave where the flock of orbs had sheltered.
    "That's weird," Code Pink commented, he stepped around the orbs as they took off from the ground.
    "What is?" Code Blue asked as they reached the entrance to the cave.
    "I had my suspicions that these were part of Red's illusions," Code Pink said as he looked at the Abysmals below.
    "No, they're real," Red's voice called out.

The Red Promethean laughed as she revealed herself directly in front of the others. Before Pink could react, Red's hand thrust forward like a blade through Pink's chest plate. Code Pink tasted blood as he spat up inside his helmet. Red still in Code Yellow's broken helmet headbutted Pink.

The force of the hit shattered both of the Promethean's helmets. The Abysmal orbs scattered from the ground as Code Pink's body dropped with a thud.

"Give me the egg," Code Red demanded, her exposed eyes twitched as she raised her hand in the air.

Code Blue who had taken the egg from Pink earlier shook her head no. Red's eye twitched as she reached down into Pink's broken mask and drove her hand into his skull.

"Just in case he's still in there," Code Red laughed, "Now, Ciela, give me the egg." Code Red raised her bloody hand out toward the Blue Promethean.

Code Black watched on as Blue turned away from the team's leader.

"You're crazy," Code Blue yelled.

Code Red stood up and approached Blue, "No, not crazy. I just see through the illusion. Give me the power to kill the Emperor and Code Gold, so that I can show the Seven Colonies true peace."

Code Blue looked at the egg in her arms and back to Code Black and knew what she had to do. Code Red was inches from Blue as she turned from Red with the egg and jumped from the cave entrance.

PONTOPPIDAN
Code Green
Revan-V

The ground shook below Code Green as the battery to Revan-V was completely drained.

I'm sorry, Little one, Code Green thought as she unplugged her wrist and put the wire away.

"Is it finished?" Code Red asked as Green climbed out from below the ship. Green dusted herself off and nodded to her leader, "It's done."

Code Red trembled with excitement.

"Get in there and fire it up," Code Red replied.

Code Green looked around and asked, "What about the others? Are they on their way?"

Code Red nodded, and said, "They're right over there."

Code Green turned to face the treeline Red had pointed to and saw another Code Red lead the full team. Code Green still had her guard up like she was in danger, but she was relieved to see the group return safely.

Code Red managed to draw a discharger from her hip holster while Green's back was turned, and fired at her. Code Green turned quickly toward Red as her energy swelled inside her. Green's eyes emitted light bright enough to shine through her visor.

    She was fast enough to extend a palm out and catch the blast from Red's discharger and absorb its energy.

    "What the hell was that?" Code Green asked, pissed that her leader attacked her.

    The Code Red that attacked Green still had the discharger focused on her, finger on the trigger. Before Red could make a move again the moon shook with a boom, followed by a huge gust of wind.

    Code Red looked around and commented to herself, "What the hell was that?" The sky above them shifted as the moon accelerated through space.

    The rest of the team regrouped with Green and Red at the ship, but Code Green saw through the illusion.

    "Stop, Red," Green demanded, "It's over."

    Code Red laughed and pulled the trigger on the discharger again.

    Code Green raised a palm again to absorb the beam while Red added, "It's over when you get in our ship and pilot us outta here." Code Red's power of illusion made the team target Green and open fire on her from every direction.

PONTOPPIDAN

Pontoppidan was awake and now off course from his original trajectory. His large tentacles stretched out to steer his massive body toward uncharted stars.

Code Blue stumbled as she ran through the foggy forest alone with the egg.

Don't look back, She told herself as she did her best not to trip.

Illusions formed around her to haunt her vision. Blue tried to keep her focus on the ground in front of her one step at a time. Faces formed in the dirt below her feet as she stepped into illusions. Arms reached out to her, and the veil of illusion twisted the sticky grass from the surface. The grass pulled Blue down to the surface of Pontoppidan.

"Give me the egg!" Code Red cried out.

Blue felt a chill go down her spine.

She found me, Code Blue thought to herself. The Blue Promethean sat up and looked around. Code Red approached Blue as she sat there, stunned on the ground. As Red walked toward Blue she demanded again for the egg.

"What are you going to do?" Code Blue asked as Red reached her.

The team's Red leader had returned to her own helmet. She stood over Code Blue on the ground with the egg.

"I'm going to use its power to change everything," Code Red cried. "There won't be Seven Colonies anymore, I'll unite them all. I'll tame this Abysmal, Pontoppidan, and he'll survive on a diet of my enemies and naysayers. Give me that egg and I can end the pain that is The Nomical Order," Code Red trembled as she ranted. "I want to consume its power!" Red shouted as she cocked back her arm to swing on Blue.

Code Blue braced herself for Red's strike but it never came. Blue relaxed her face in her helmet and opened one eye to see Code White between her and Red.

"You saved me," Code Blue cried out, realizing White had blocked Red's punch.

"I never left your side," Code White replied.

The mysterious Promethean pushed Code Red back. White's fist flew through the air to return a punch to Red, whose head formed a hand that grabbed Code White. Red contorted through illusion, giving her leverage to throw White over her shoulder. White hit the ground but phased below the surface. Code Red looked around for White's attack.

"Blue, please run," Code White cried out from the ground at Red's feet.

Code Blue watched her love rise up from the ground to fight Red as she processed White's pleas.

53

The Blue Promethean got to her feet and turned back to see White once more. Code White saw her leave and knew there wasn't a reason to hold back anymore.

    Code Red laughed and created two clones of herself to fight Code White. Code White dematerialized before the trio of Reds could strike. A materialized fist reached out from the void and knocked a Red off her feet. The other two jumped on the area where the hand stood. The two Reds fell into each other on the ground as White materialized a few feet from them. The two Reds merged into one large body with multiple legs and long arms with blades at the hands. Red's monstrous form stood almost eight feet tall. The Red beast picked up the body of the third Red, which merged into the illusion.

    "What the-" Code White commented as Red's large scythe arm swung down on White's shoulder.

    The Promethean dematerialized at the shoulder to split in two. Red's scythe passed between the two halves of White untouched. White's shoulder and arm dropped toward the ground but were caught and reconnected. White's body finalized its materialization as Red swung again. This time Code White simply let Red phase through. As the arm went through, White stepped in closer to the beast of a form Red had assumed. Code White jumped onto Red's large body and pulled her to the ground by the neck.

As White pummeled Red they looked around for Blue, who had managed to escape. White couldn't help but feel that Blue was still in danger, and paused to look again.

Code White's vision fogged as a young woman appeared from the shadows.

"Ciela?" Code White called out. The woman shook her head and placed a hand on White's chest.

"Have you forgotten me?" The young woman asked. Code White was overwhelmed with memories. Memories from their time together on Promethean, when White was Code Silver. She was the daughter of General Gold, and Code Silver was second in command of the Prometheans.

"I never forgot you," Code White cried out, "Not after what Gold did to you. I haven't been able to connect to anyone since you were taken from me." Code White looked down to the ground at their feet.

"Look at me," The woman replied.

Code White was too focused on Blue to respond.

"Look at me!" The woman called out again.

When Code White looked up the woman was solid gold.

"You did this to me," she accused Code White, "You touched the General's daughter, and look what happened!"

Code White cried out as the memories came back.

This is just an illusion, Code White thought. The woman moved closer to Code White who raised a hand in response.

White's fist hung frozen in the air, with blood-soaked knuckles. White looked to the left and to the right.

"Where is she?" Code White screamed.

Code Red laughed uncontrollably through the fog of her illusion.

"You mean you can't see her?" Code Red mocked White, "She's right here."

Code Red laughed again as White turned back to her, "Where is she?"

Code White screamed again. "I can -feel her," White cried out, "Why can I feel her presence?"

"Because," Red replied, her voice changed to a more familiar one, "Because- I've been here all along," Blue said.

Red's illusion faded to reveal Code Blue on the other end of White's assault.

"No," Code White cried out and dropped to the ground beside a bloody and beaten Blue. "My Sapphire," White whispered to Blue with hands soaked in her blood.

"We should have picked out a nice planet for ourselves at the auction houses," Blue chuckled in a weak voice. Code White pulled her in closer and removed her battered helmet.

"I'm sorry," White whispered over and over.

"Don't be," Code Blue replied to her love, "It was worth it to me just to touch you, and to finally know you, Lo." Code White pulled off his helmet to stare into Blue's eyes with his own.

"Don't fade away from me," Code White cried, as Blue died in his arms.

Code Red, now in possession of the egg, watched White scream in pain from the safety of the trees. Red's only window to escape would soon be over as Pontoppidan approached Crude Space.

PONTOPPIDAN

Code Green
Revan-V

Code Green redirected some of the energy fired at her back at Code Red.

"That's all you got?" Code Green yelled as she unleashed a blast of energy of her own she had stored.

Green's attack was strong enough to vaporize Red's illusion, as the team Red created faded too. Code Green sighed and cursed to herself.

"Guess that was all you got," Green said before she turned back to the ship. The real Code Red stood at the door to Revan-V, with the egg.

"So, this is the last time we gotta do this?" Code Green asked Red as she approached the leader at the ship. Code Red held up the egg to show Green.

"Time after time humanity rebuilds from the farthest edges of extinction," Red noted. The Promethean gripped the egg in her hand and cracked it open.

"With this, we'll rebuild it all in my image," Red laughed as the egg broke open.

Liquid metal dripped from inside the shell in Red's hand.

"Devmetal?" Red gasped with delight, "Do you realize what this egg is?"

Code Green saw the egg and mustered up all the charged energy stored in her body. In one swift move Code Green raised her arms toward Revan-V and unleashed a bolt of energy toward the ship. The explosion engulfed Red and the egg, reaching Code Green as well. She absorbed the energy put off by the blast, but shrapnel shredded Green's body. As she fell to the ground surrounded by flames Code Black appeared before her.

"You made it," Code Green said in a weak voice.

"You didn't have to blow up the ship, Kiwa," Code Black replied.

"I-I know," Code Green laughed, "But I didn't know who to trust, and I didn't want the ship to be misused."

Code Black stood up from the debris around himself and Code Green. He had seen enough, and Pontoppidan would hit Crude Space any minute.

"Red, are you still out there?" Code Black yelled out.

A gust of wind left the burning hull of the ship and blew past Code Black, who didn't flinch. Code Red emerged in the flames, and stepped through the inferno, for a standoff with Black.

"I still have the egg," Code Red cried out. "I win," Red laughed as she held up a fragment of the shell.

"What was it, anyway?" Code Black asked.

Black looked to the sky as stars continued to streak by.
     "It's infinite possibilities," Code Red said.
     The twisted leader held up a small slug-like creature.
     "This is the embryo of an Astronomical, the gods of Crude Space, and its power will be mine," Code Red remarked.
     The undeveloped alien squirmed while Red removed her helmet with her free hand.
     "Now, the fun begins," Code Red said as she raised the small life-form above her head.
     She dropped the slug into her mouth. As she chewed, Red's veins in her face began to glow, while the ground below them shook. Pontoppidan crashed through the cosmic atmosphere created by The Nomical Order. The sky above Red and Black filled with vibrant colors as they entered Crude Space. Code Black watched reality around Red begin to shift as her power grew to Astronomical scale.
     "It's over, Red," Code Black yelled out to his fellow Promethean.
     "I am a god," Code Red commented on the power that raged inside her body.
     "Still," Red confessed, "I can't escape this phantom pain cursed upon me by the previous Code Black. No matter, I'll kill another Code Black before I kill all the other Prometheans back home."

Code Red turned her attention to Code Black in the distance among the flames.

"It is over, for you," Code Red laughed as she lunged for Code Black. Red reached her target with force but passed through him.

"What is this?" Code Red demanded as she turned back towards Code Black.

"So, phantom pain, huh," Code Black remarked to Red, "And you feel everything?"

Code Red was confused by Black's interest in her condition, "Yeah, that's right," Red began, "I killed Code Black. But that bastard used his ability to make me feel the pain of everything I've ever experienced. My limbs are constantly numb, and they're aching all the time."

"That must be hard on you," Black said, as Red swung at him again, "But why kill your teammate?"

"It's excruciating," Red remarked, as her second attempt to hit Black failed.

"I killed Code Black because his power rivaled mine. General Gold had made threats of promoting him to PROTO Rank." The Prometheans faced off with each other as Red's body swelled with power.

"So your pride killed him?" Code Black questioned.

"Can I tell you the truth?" Code Black asked as Red swung at him again, still unable to hit him.

Red's frustration grew with each failed strike, "What are you?" Red yelled out.

Code Black took a step toward Code Red.

"I'm-" Code Black started but corrected himself, "My name is AP. As in Astral Projection, you see, I'm not really here right now."

Code Red was startled, "Doesn't matter where you are. I'll find you, and kill you like the others," Red promised, "My powers will soon reach across all the known cosmos." Code Black looked around them as the stars raced by above their heads.

"I don't think so," Code Black commented, "See, It's not where I am you should be worried about, I'm aboard Revan-V by the way. No, it's a matter of when."

Code Red stared at Black and asked, "When?"

Code Black nodded, "I can project my spirit across the perceived planes of time. I can visit anywhere I've been or will end up going. I've seen enough. General Gold allowed me to join your unit to investigate the previous Code Black's death. Now if you don't mind, this alarm has been driving me nuts." Code Black faded away as Code Red stepped toward him.

Code Red cried out as the energy that raged within her body engulfed her. Elsewhere Code White still clung to the body of his love as Pontoppidan laughed to himself. The Abysmal wrapped himself in his long tentacles to drift back to sleep within Crude Space.

PIUS COLONY
Revan-V Mid Drift

"Code Black!"

"You just gonna ignore that back there?" Code Yellow called from the seat ahead.

"Code Black!"

The unit shuffled from frustration in their seats as Code black struggled.

"First time?" Code Green called out.

Code Black chuckled, then replied, "Something like that."

"Code Black!"

The cockpit was alive with frustration as Code Green chimed in, "Greenhorn, want me to Bypass it?" Her emerald visor reflected back toward Code Black.

Black let out a sigh and placed a finger on the touch display for confirmation, and called out, "I got it." His astral form had returned to his body, which meant he could interact with the physical plane again.

VII STARMETRO

"Damn, what an entanglement!" Topaz Jack laughed as his helmet gushed smoke clouds.

"Don't take it the wrong way, but if it wasn't for this guy," Topaz pointed toward Black, "you'd all be screwed."

When the ship landed the Promethean team was greeted by royal guards that arrested Code Red. Topaz Jack sat beside General Gold as the team was debriefed.

"We're classifying this mission, of course," General Gold declared. "The six of you will head back home to Promethean until your next assignment."

White and Blue excused themselves from the celebration to explore the auction houses. Code Green sat with Black while Pink and Yellow went to gamble.

"That was a big risk," Code Green said as she leaned over the rail of the balcony they were on.

"What do you think will happen next?" Green asked.

Code Black looked out over the rail of the balcony to view StarMetro's casinos.

"I don't know," Black confided in Green.

He stared at the horizon and let out a sigh, then added, "But now I can rest knowing my brother's killer has been found."

Code Green placed her hand on Black's back and said, "I loved him, too. That's why you came to me with your plan in the first place. His love connects us, so you know I'll always have your back, okay?"

•••

The next morning as Code Black loaded the ship, General Gold approached him.

"Good morning, son," Gold greeted Black. Code Black stood straight and saluted the General.

"That's not necessary right now," The General remarked.

"You look good in Black, Reject, looks like we were wrong about you. You earned your spot among the Prometheans. Now, get your bags off that ship. Your presence is being requested elsewhere, Code Black," The General laughed.

Code Black was happy to no longer be a Reject but unsure why he wouldn't be with his fellow Prometheans.

"Don't just stand there, son," The General added, "Emperor Yujen has requested to meet you back on Octavian."

Code Black felt a familiar lump form in his throat, "W-why me," Code Black questioned.

General Gold placed a hand on Black's shoulder, "Don't overthink it, son. I'm sure he just wants to meet the Prometheans that discovered Pontoppidan." General Gold turned to leave.

"Excuse me," Code Black asked, "But you said Prometheans, and I never briefed you on Pontoppidan."

Code Black's curiosity grew as the General stopped, looked back, and added, "Right. Well, Yujen wants to meet you and the other team we sent to retrieve the weapon. You didn't entirely hold up your end of the deal. Your mission was to get intel on the moon but you failed to mention Pontoppidan by name or the Astronomical egg."

Code Black blurted out, "You sent another team without knowing what they'd find? What if someone on that team went rogue too?"

The General stood silent then added, "Get your things ready. Once we reach Octavian I'll get to see our new Promethean Moon, Pontoppidan, firsthand.

Emperor Yujen's given us the moon since he plans to hatch the Astronomical egg for himself. He'll use its power to eradicate his enemies within the Aurelius Colony. After that Pax Armata will be certain, as the remaining Colonies fall in line. Can I trust you to do the same?"

Code Black remained quiet. The General took his silence as obedience and left Code Black alone outside Revan-V.

Code Black paused to look at his bags in the storage and thought about his home Colony Aurelius, and his brother. After a short pause, Code Black had formed a plan and left his bags to find Code Green.

ZANE PALMER

End of Crude Space
Part I

CRUDE SPACE

CRUDE SPACE
SILVER SANCTION

ZANE PALMER

CRUDE SPACE: SILVER SANCTION

INTRO

The time has come for peace to reign. The Augustus Colony is preparing to declare Pax Armata in an effort to maintain order. **The Nomical Order** remains divided over the fate of the Seven Colonies of Man. On the Eve of Victory, Emperor Yujen calls for a Celebration to commemorate the end of an era ravaged by war.

Deep within the Vespasian Colony, Code Silver of the Prometheans escorts his subordinates. The eight PROs in protective custody are on a one-way trip to the capital world Octavian to meet the Emperor. One Officer among them, Code Black, has not taken to the invitation well and harbors an agenda of his own. Distracted by ego, Code Silver has been unaware of another ship, the Revan-V, tracking them.

Meanwhile, two tired **Prometheans** arrive at their new world near the other side of the galaxy. But even in their lonely region imbalance finds them, as access to a nearby star proves difficult.

VIII VESPASIAN COLONY
Pope-I Mid Drift

Code Silver meditated in his seat as Code Green of the CIVth unit piloted them towards Octavian. The second in command of the Prometheans hated traveling through the Vespasian Colony. As he meditated memories of his early life there returned to him. Code Silver thought about the one memory he had of his father, Manzh, who he received his name from.

His father was absent for most of his early years. The men on Manzh's homeworld had been drafted to construct the former Emperor's palace. Vespasians had a reputation for being the most skilled builders in the Seven Colonies of Man.

One day his father returned home when Manzh was just a young boy living with his mother in a small village. His mother screamed when she saw that her spouse had lost a hand. Manzh ran to his father crying and offered a hand of his own. His father laughed at him and picked little Manzh up with his good arm as he continued to cry. His father was unaware that Manzh had the ability to heal himself instantaneously. Manzh's father returned to work the following day, and his mother got the news later of his passing.

Manzh saw the completed Palace for the first time after he took on the role of Code Silver of the Prometheans. As his thoughts shifted to the palace and the Emperor, Manzh focused on his personal mission. His determination left a tremble in his hands as he crossed his arms.

POPE-1
Mess Hall
Code Black

"Stop touching me!" Code Black cried out. He sat between two other Prometheans with his back against the cold wall of the ship's mess hall. His arms were crossed against his armored chest with a feeding tube connected to his wrist.

On his left was Code White, and on his right sat a second Code Black. The two belonged to the unit of Prometheans that managed to capture Pontoppidan. Across from them was Code Yellow from the same unit.

"Stop touching me!" Code Black cried out again. He grabbed the small hand of the second Code Black and moved it away from his chest.

Code Yellow sighed as this continued. The mechanical pumps connected to their wrists continued spewing nutrients into their bodies. There was a low-pitched hum produced by the ship's worn-out mechanics that no one could ignore.

"We gotta make sure you don't astral project anywhere," Code White commented. The Promethean leaned back away from Code Black. A tap landed on Code White's left shoulder causing the Promethean to jump and look to see nothing there to cause it.

"That's not going to stop me from astral projecting," Code Black replied.

The other Code Black placed a palm on Code Black's chest and the two of them were suddenly across the mess hall. "That's okay, AP," the second Code Black said, "We'd escape from this together if I could teleport beyond my line of sight." AP shook his head to shake off the sensation of teleporting. He never imagined that it would make him so dizzy. The second Code Black returned to the table to clean up the mess made by teleporting out of their feeding tubes.

"So, you guys realize what this mission is?" AP, Code Black, asked. Code Yellow nodded and motioned for AP to approach.

"We know," Code Yellow replied, "And that's why we want to make the most of it." The yellow Promethean extended a hand outward toward AP, who accepted. The Promethean felt a static feeling go up his arm and radiate through his body. Before AP could let go of Code Yellow's hand he was levitating into the air.

AP began to experience motion sickness as he closed his eyes to project his spirit below himself. He reached out and grabbed his own hand, pulling his body back down and placing his feet on the floor. As AP's out-of-body experience ended Code Yellow remarked, "Never seen anyone do that. Normally they just get stuck on the ceiling."

AP gave Code Yellow a cold stare that could be felt through their helmets. "We don't have time for jokes," AP stated. The Promethean found a new seat at the table that was separated from the rest of the group.

"I don't know why you're so worried about them when I'm the most powerful Promethean," Code White laughed. Code Yellow and the other Code Black scoffed.

AP replied, "Spare me any demonstrations, and just tell me what you do, maybe we can help each other later."

Code White looked down and sighed. "Well," the White Promethean began, "I become denser. Basically, you could crash a ship into me and it would bounce right off." Code White's two teammates became visibly irritated. AP thought that was a very specific choice of words but brushed it off.

"Right," AP replied, "What does the rest of your unit do?" AP leaned forward with his elbows on the table. The three other Prometheans looked at one another and then back at AP.

"Well, Code Red can hypnotize you. But you have to look at the hand gesture they make in order for it to work," Code Yellow began.

"Code Green is like a power amp, our abilities are stronger around Green. Code Blue is a Seer, that's how we watched your team fail to capture Pontopiddan," Code Yellow continued. AP smiled under his helmet. He had felt someone looking over his shoulder during his previous mission. It felt as if someone was reading his every move. Even now, AP felt that same feeling as he sat with his fellow officers.

"So was that how your unit captured Pontopiddan? You saw what we did, and did the opposite?" AP asked. Code White nodded as Yellow continued.

"That's part of it. Our Code Pink is an animal talker, we combined that with Red's hypnotism and linked Pontoppidan to you, AP. As long as you were acting out your mission in the astral plane Pontoppidan would be there with you. Well, his consciousness would be, that is," Code Yellow concluded.

AP nodded as he processed the information. "So you forced Pontopiddan's mind into the astral plane? Do I have that right?" AP questioned.

Code Yellow nodded and said, "That's how we understand it, yes. Code Blue mentioned that your Blue woke Pontopiddan and that you made contact. What was that like?"

AP ignored Code Blue's question and asked, "You didn't wake Pontopiddan?"

The three Prometheans shook their heads no. AP was surprised to learn this information. If Pontopiddan was still asleep under Promethean control, perhaps he could be freed. AP's mind was formulating a plan to save Pontopiddan. Unfortunately, he wasn't even in a position to save himself. His only comfort was knowing that Code Green piloting the Revan-V would be on their trail by now. That was all that mattered.

IX CLAUDIUS COLONY

Dwarf Planet
Code Blue and White

    Ciela held Lo's hand as the two stepped off of the small shuttle that brought them down to the surface of the planet. Their Promethean helmets were packed away in the bags draped over their backs. The shuttle ascended back into space as the wind swept up a dust cloud around the two Prometheans.
    "We made it," Ciela cheered. She could feel Lo's emotions through their embrace and shared his relief.
    "Let's find a place to make camp before nightfall," Lo remarked. The White Promethean had let his guard down after their last mission. For years he had become so consumed with the anger and guilt that came with causing his first love's death.
    Code Black had warned Lo about the culmination of that guilt resulting in the astral death of Code Blue. After taking a leave from the Prometheans, Lo and Ciela bought a planet at auction that they could make into a home.
    Now on that humid dwarf planet, the two Prometheans trekked across the countryside. The nearby star shined brightly on the horizon beyond the hills at their backs.

"This planet orbits that star once every four galactic years," Ciela commented. The two continued for a few minutes before Lo replied, "Have you figured out what we're going to name this place?"

Ciela shrugged and then said, "We've got plenty of time to figure that out before we head back to Promethean."

Lo smiled at her and then added, "We should settle here for the night. Tomorrow we can find those rivers we saw before landing." They worked together to set up a tent using tools from their bags. As the star settled over the hills and night came Ciela and Lo heard a thunderous noise approaching. Lo phased through their tent to see dozens of aliens crowded around them. Their species was unfamiliar to Lo and Ciela, as were the creatures they rode.

"Hello," Lo said. He had removed his armor and gotten comfortable moments before they arrived. The two of them were completely surrounded.

"Howdy," One of the riders greeted, as his mount stepped forward. The aliens were noticeably shorter than Lo and Ciela, no bigger than a human child. They had long feathers growing along their arms and underneath the armor on their legs. Their faces resembled humans but had two sets of nostrils along the bridge of their noses. Some of their faces were decorated with piercings that reflected in the dark.

The hairy creatures they rode were headless with beastly faces between their shoulders. Their front arms were sturdy like tree trunks.
    Lo scanned the terrestrials around him and noticed none of them held weapons of any kind.
    "Are you friendly?" Lo called out. The rider that stepped forward in the crowd approached the Prometheans. He had a distinct piercing through the bridge of his nose, and his feathers were an amber color.
    "Friendly? Heck, we're family now that you folks bought this land. My name's Senk." He declared. The group nodded along and raised their right hand to pat their left shoulder twice like it was a salute.
    Ciela approached Lo and Senk and waved to the group.
    "I'm Ciela, and this is Lo, We're Pro-" Ciela began to introduce them but Lo cut her off. "We're settling this planet," Lo interrupted. Ciela was unsure why Lo was hiding who they were from the inhabitants.
    "We've been expecting you, Prometheans," Senk replied, "Now get your things and come with us."

VESPASIAN COLONY

Pope-I
Crossing the Border into Augustus
Code Silver

As Code Green piloted the Pope-I out of the Vespasian Colony Manzh remained in meditation. His mind journeyed through his academic years on Promethean with his friends Lo and Brek. Their abilities made them stand out and gain instant consideration for PROTO rankings. Manzh and his friends had even competed to claim the title of Code Silver. The outcome of that competition led to Lo's Sanctioning as Code Silver. Manzh had carried a chip on his shoulder that remained for years. Despite this, the two maintained their friendship until the day Lo lost his way and broke his oath.

"Sir, I Don't mean to wake you, but we'll be arriving at Octavian sooner than expected," Code Green remarked.

Manzh shook his head to clear the memories of his battle with Lo years ago. He could still hear the screams from that woman as the General turned her into a golden statue to punish Lo.

"Thank you," Manzh replied. He was Code Silver, he reminded himself. He eased his mind out of the past and back into the present. He had a mission to complete.

Octavian was a beautiful manmade planet created in the image of mankind's first world. The Pope-I broke through the atmosphere as the two manmade moons of the planet crossed in the skyline. Skyscrapers and towering buildings covered every inch of the sprawling landscape. Crystal-clear waters filtered by the planet itself made up the massive oceanic regions.

The Small craft of PROs traveled through the largest city in the Nomical Order, Olymzes. Emperor Yujen's Palace was at the center of it all. The building was built high into the clouds, with several towers spaced out so far they were a blur. Gold laced the entire structure, a gift from the General who had served since Zemula's time on the throne.

Manzh hated this Palace but it allowed him to visit his father. The Silver Promethean looked out from the ship to see a set of windows he imagined his father falling from. He never found out what exactly happened to his father, and it had been nearly as long since he'd seen his mother.

As the Pope-I landed on the rooftop dock Manzh noticed the General's ship hadn't arrived yet. Dozens of ships belonging to senators and kings of the Nomical Order were unloading.

Manzh stood from his seat after Code Green deactivated the ship's engines. This is it, Manzh thought to himself, everyone on this ship must be feeling the same way.

"PROTO Green," Code Silver called out. Code Green stood at attention and awaited Silver's command.

"Retrieve your unit and prepare them for the Emperor," Manzh ordered.

X CLAUDIUS COLONY

Dwarf Planet
Code Blue and White

"Lo and Ciela rode with the inhabitants of their new world through nightfall and into the morning. The two Prometheans sat together on the back of one of the strange beasts provided to them. The animal ran at a steady pace, grunting through each stride. Senk and his people hadn't said much since the two PROs packed their lives again to travel with them. Around midday, they crossed through a valley of sapling trees and emerged on the other side by a village.

"This is us," Senk called out. The riders alongside him began to cheer and raise their right hands into the air to slap their shoulders. The villagers came out of their mud and thatch huts in droves to greet their returning neighbors. Ciela smiled seeing the adolescent ones climb onto the beasts their fathers rode to hug them. These are kind people, Ciela thought. She had scanned the history of the beast she rode, a toar, as the locals called them. The memories of alien lifeforms were harder to piece together but Ciela saw happy ones from her toar. Lo climbed down from their mount and helped Ciela down after him.

His hesitancy to touch her had become a thing of the past as he continued to hold her hand after she was on solid ground.

Senk dismounted his toar and hugged his loved ones before finding Lo and Ciela.

"You have a lot of offspring," Ciela commented as the feathered father approached. Senk smiled and looked back at the seven children walking with their mother. When he turned back to them his smile had faded.

"Thanks," Senk replied, "Used to be more of 'em, but the winter years here can be brutal." Ciela wanted to reach out to Senk and comfort him but she held back to avoid the memories of the loss he had endured.

"You two must be tired from your journey," Senk said, changing the subject, "Please allow me to show you to your new home." The two Prometheans walked with Senk down the rocky roads of their village. Some of the locals who volunteered to carry their belongings followed close behind. They stopped in the center of the village at a large building made of large dark stones. Besides the roads, it was the only thing in the village not made of mud and thrash.

"This is beautiful," Ciela remarked, staring up at the craftsmanship. Lo nodded along to agree with her. Senk turned back to them with a proud smile.

"It's yours," Senk said through his grin. The villagers carrying the Promethean's belongings did not stop with them. Instead, they proceeded into the building ahead of Lo and Ciela to drop off the PRO's bags.

The two Prometheans looked at one another and then back at Senk before Ciela replied, "We can't accept this. It's more than we need." Senk's smile sank into concern as he said, "Nonsense, this was built for the two of you. Some of us tore down our homes to make this space here for you upon your arrival." The villagers had finished setting up inside the home and returned to the three outside.

"What's the problem, is it too small?" One of the women who had volunteered questioned.

Senk turned to his neighbors and said, "No, they say it's too much space. They don't need it."

The woman squawked back, "What?" As she continued to chirp the group joined her. They continued as Senk began to shout back at them, creating a ruckus.

Ciela and Lo shared a glance again as if they both couldn't believe what they were hearing. Ciela smiled at Lo and then stepped toward the flock of bickering aliens before her.

"Calm down, Calm down," Ciela cried out. The locals stopped yapping long enough for Ciela to speak. "Thank you for our new home, everyone," She shouted to the group.

Senk's grin grew wider than ever as the aliens cheered. Lo and Ciela Thanked them with a bow. The aliens returned the gesture by doing their shoulder salute. "This calls for a celebration!" Senk declared, "We'll let you rest but please welcome us into your home tonight. We'll leave you now so that we can prepare the finest dishes for your pleasure."

Lo and Ciela were hungry after their trip and sudden departure with the aliens. The two Prometheans agreed to the dinner plans without hesitation.

CLAUDIUS COLONY
Dwarf Planet
Inside Code Blue and White's Home

That evening as Ciela and Lo settled into the world they purchased at auction, a party was held at their new home. Senk introduced Lo and Ciela to his wife, Kernne, as well as the village elders. Large tables of food were arranged on each wall of the room they gathered in. Ciela could feel Lo's frustration without using her ability as the crowd of locals grew. The two Prometheans had hoped to build their relationship on this planet but so far they hadn't had time to do that. Their scheduled time away from Promethean was limited and they would soon have to return. Ciela worried that Lo might be regretting their decision now that they were there on their own world.

To Ciela's surprise, Lo was quick to warm up to the local aliens as their home filled with neighbors. They sat at a round table near the center of the room with Senk and Kernne, where they were joined by Senk's cousin. As Senk's raven-feathered cousin sat down Ciela noticed his forehead was tattooed.

"This is my cousin, Garude," Senk said. He held a hand out to greet Garude, who accepted it. Lo and Ciela waved from their side of the table and said,

"Hello." Garude's stature was much larger than the others, but he sank low into his seat with his head held low.

"Is this them?" Garude questioned Senk, motioning to the Prometheans across from them. Senk nodded, and said, "Now that you're here we can begin."

Begin what? Ciela thought as she watched Garude signal towards a woman near the doors. A moment later a group of children came out decorated in feathers designed to look like armor. They filled up the empty space in the center of the room as the lights dimmed low. What's happening? Ciela wondered as she looked over at Lo beside her. His eyes were lasered in on the theatrics.

There was a pause as one of the children stepped forward wearing dark feathers. The child looked around the room nervously before making contact with Ciela. They smiled at each other momentarily as the child's attention shifted to Senk and Kernne. The three exchanged an excited wave before the child spoke up, "Ahem- I am the great warrior Garude." The child's voice was shaky at first.

"That's one of my boys," Senk whispered across the table to Ciela and Lo. Ciela gave a polite nod but then worried that her expression lacked interest.

The boy continued, "Years ago our peaceful race known as Uzalech came to roost on this tiny planet. Our elders migrated here just as our species has done every generation since the dawn of Lech."

The other children ran around the boy in circles, making whooshing noises. "But then one day, He came." The boy shouted. He threw his hands up over his head and continued, "The wicked demon from the sky who blocked out the sky, the Sunriza."

The crowd gasped and booed at the Boy presenting. The other children continued to circle around him as he lowered his arms. The lights focused on the center of the room went dark. Another child stepped forward out of the darkness wearing dark robes.

"I am the Sunriza," the robed boy declared, "And I have come to claim your star, and your people as mine." The crowd booed louder at the boy. Ciela looked over at Lo who was mesmerized by the tale.

"No, you can't make us be your prisoners here forever!" The boy dressed as Garude cried out. He ran across the room as the lights grew brighter. The two boys pretended to fight as the other children joined in, dogpiling on top of the boy acting as the Sunriza. The crowd cheered.

"I am dead," The child acting as the Sunriza cried out from the ground.

"He is dead," Senk's son acting as Garude cried out as he stood over the other boy. The crowd of Uzalech cheered from their seats before standing to salute. The children saluted back as the actor playing the Sunriza continued to play dead. As the cheers continued the lights dimmed to allow the children to clear the area.

"So, what'd ya think?" Senk asked as the lights cut back on. Lo glanced over to Ciela who was speechless. The white Promethean glanced back over to Senk sitting opposite of him.

"Your kid has great acting skills. But my question is, is that all true?" Lo remarked.

Garude scoffed from his side of the table and answered, "Those kids embellished." He picked up his drink and looked away taking a swig.

Ciela poked at the plate of worms Kernne served her. There was a mix of cooked and live worms moving about on her plate as she lost her appetite. They traveled with feeding tubes that she had upstairs in their room that she would connect to later.

"Don't listen to my cousin, even if he is our greatest hero," Senk said. He looked over to Garude who refused to acknowledge everyone at the table. "He's dealing with survivor's guilt," Senk continued.

Garude's drink splashed from his cup as he slammed it down on the table. His stare zeroed in on Senk as he shouted, "You think it's heroic to get others killed? Do you know what it feels like to turn into a killer yourself?" Garude shouted. The room fell silent. Senk stood and approached Garude to apologize, saying, "I'm sorry, Gar, I didn't know." He wrapped a feathered arm around his cousin, who pushed him aside. Garude stood and stormed out of the room without a word.

Suddenly the room fell dark again. A young voice shouted out, "Now that we have your attention, we want to thank you and welcome you, our new Gods." A beam of light shined down again on Senk's son, dressed as Garude. "For you will be the ones to rule over us, and protect us against any and all harm," The boy continued.

Senk cleared his throat, which was loud enough to echo through the room. He then motioned for them to stop as the lights cut back on and his son ran back out of sight.

"What was that?" Ciela asked. Lo was curious as well and asked, "Yeah, what was that part about new Gods?"

Senk chuckled nervously as he thought of an answer. "The thing is," Senk began, "We sold our planet because we figured whoever bought it was rich enough to keep us safe. You see, we were stuck here for a long time because of the Sunriza, and we're broke."

Ciela gave Lo a look and then asked, "Is that why you've been treating us like royalty? You think we're here to be your saviors?"

Senk looked around the room at his family and fellow Uzalech, and said, "Well, yeah. you're Prometheans, right? When we found out who bought our planet at auction we figured you were coming to help." The crowd mumbled and nodded along with Senk's words.

Ciela never imagined that the rest of the Nomical Order felt that way about Prometheans. They were a force for order not necessarily good, at least that's what General Gold taught them.

"We don't have much to offer you by ourselves," Lo told the Uzalech. "We don't plan on staying on this world very long," The white Promethean stated, "When we leave we can have aid sent to you. There's a shuttle that will pick us up soon and take us to the Claudian Port for the Hyper-Train. They might even let some of you aboard the shuttle so you can speak to the Senate and ask for aid" Lo informed the Uzalech.

The people chattered amongst themselves at each table as they weighed their options.

"So, you're not here to rule, and you want us to ask for the help of the Nomical Order?" Senk asked from across the table.

"That's right," Lo said, adding, "I'm sorry, but we weren't expecting this when we bought your planet."

Ciela looked around the room at all the concerned faces.

"The Nomical Order doesn't care about the Uzalech," Senk declared, "But if they are our only hope then we must ask them." Senk looked around the room for reassurance from his community and found it on each of their faces.

The doors to the room burst open as Garude returned to the party. His raven feathers had taken a lighter shade and stood up on his neck and head extending from his body. He had produced talons from his feet, hands, knees, elbows, and shoulders. His beastly form caused the room of Uzalech to screech and flap their feathered arms. Senk ran to the open space in the center of the room to face his cousin.

"Garude, what is the meaning of this?" Senk demanded. His amber feathers stood up as Ciela and Lo watched on. The two cousins hissed at each other as they bared their teeth.

"Cousin," Garude hissed, "I am not here to cause trouble, but it has once again appeared on our doorstep." Ciela and Lo stood and approached the two Uzalech in their standoff.

"What's going on?" Lo asked. Garude lowered his arms but his talons remained exposed.

"Come outside, and see it in the night sky for yourselves," Garude said. He stepped aside as Senk led Lo and Ciela out the door and into the open air. The Uzalech villagers crowded around them outside of the Promethean's massive home.

"What are we looking for?" Ciela asked as she scanned the darkness over them. Lo looked around in the sky as well but could not see anything.

"It can't be," Senk cried. The amber-feathered Uzalech glanced over to his cousin. Garude hesitated to nod and confirm Senk's fears. "You two can't see it in the dark with your human eyes, but there's another planet, an unnatural one, up there," Senk said. He pointed a finger to the sky as the two Prometheans followed its path up into nothing. "He calls his massive flat planet his Sunviza," Senk added, swallowing the lump in his throat. The crowd of Uzalech was in an uproar as they cried out.

"Who?" Ciela asked.

Garude continued to stare into the sky as he nodded and said, "The Sunriza. If his planet is back it can only mean that he's back. He uses his Sunviza to block us out from all contact."

"What does that mean?" Lo questioned. Senk turned to him and replied, "Mean's we can kiss that shuttle of yours goodbye. That's not the worst of it though. He's blocked us out from using his star, meaning it's going to get real cold, fast."

Ciela frowned as she grabbed Lo's hand. She could tell that he was feeling the same as her through their contact. Lo looked over at her and said, "We can handle this." Ciela nodded to him as Senk interrupted, and asked, "Does this mean you'll help us?" The crowd around them stared at the two Prometheans as they awaited their answer.

Ciela looked at Lo for his approval then nodded to Senk to confirm their choice to help. The crowd cheered them on. Garude approached them and placed a taloned hand on Lo's shoulder.

"We can do this together," Garude promised. His confidence ignited the crowd around them.

Ciela smiled and turned to Lo and said, "I know what we're going to name this planet."

"What's that?" Lo asked as he stared into Ciela's eyes. She smiled and looked up at the starless night sky and replied, "We're going to name our planet Estrella."

XI AUGUSTUS COLONY
Olymzyes, Octavian
Emperor Yujen's Palace
Royal Colosseum Guest Hall

In Over one thousand Nomical authorities had gathered to commemorate Emperor Yujen's proclamation. After years of planting the seeds of peace within the Nomical Order, they were coming to fruition. Every politician and nobleman from the Seven Colonies sat eagerly awaiting Yujen's arrival.

The Emperor's guests were packed into the colosseum when Code Silver entered. The colosseum they were in held hundreds of hexagonal platforms of various heights. An elevator shaft at the base of each one led to a private sky box above.

Code Green from the CIVth unit followed Silver along with Code Black from the CVIIth unit. Behind the two of them were the six other PROs from the CIVth unit. Code Silver had placed them all under arrest the moment the ship docked. His mission was to deliver the PROs directly affiliated with Pontopiddan here tonight. He wasn't sure why, or what General Gold planned on doing with them. He still hadn't seen Gold since they arrived but he kept his eye out for their leader. The Prometheans had a special table in a box near the Emperors.

The elevator ride to the top was quiet as Silver stood amongst the PROs on their way to uncertainty. Code Silver's attention was on Code Black from the CVIIth. Something about the PRO felt familiar to Manzh.

When they stepped out of the elevator they had a better view of the Palace from above the Colosseum. Their box sat high above the city of Olymzes below. A golden dome sat several stories above, with an open skyline visible in every direction.

Manzh found a silver chair sitting beside a golden throne at the table. He ordered the PROs in his custody to take their seats around the table. Code Black from the CVIIth unit sat across from Manzh with Code White on his left and Code Yellow on his right. The long table between them had the distinct craftsmanship of a Vespasian designer.

Code Silver spread his gloved hands out over the table to admire the material it was made of. His Silver helmet held back the mixed emotions he had for the locale. He found a feeding tube ready for him at the table and plugged it in to distract himself. His gaze turned to the stars above them. There was a chill in the air at their altitude. He enjoyed it but still found himself pulling his silver sash closer to his neck and chest for warmth.

With his helmet still fixed on the sky Manzh turned his attention to the PROs at the table from the corner of his eye. They had been unusually quiet since their arrest.

As second in command, Manzh was familiar with arresting his subordinates. He had firsthand knowledge of the number of Prometheans General Gold went through. The code stated that they would maintain seven units, consisting of seven officers. Those units always came back with one hundred percent success rates on missions. General Gold saw to it that the Prometheans maintained a positive public image. The Prometheans were stripped of their identities beyond their Colony of origin.

They were placed inside a helmet and given new names, that was their first Promethean code.

When Manzh joined the Prometheans he was an eager child ready to fight bad guys and save worlds. His fame and fortune never came but he learned the hard way after years of beatings that he was a survivor. No matter what he came up against he could survive its wrath. He had survived his battle with Lo to take the Silver moniker. His reasons for never giving up led him to become Code Yellow of the LXXVIIth unit, then Code Silver. Now after years in his role as second in command, Manzh envisioned more for himself.

The elevator door behind them in their skybox began to ding. Manzh and the PRO prisoners stood as General Gold, leader of the Prometheans emerged. The Promethean was decorated with Golden robes and a long cape on his back. His golden helmet swiveled back and forth as he scanned the nine PROs before him.

General Gold removed his hands from inside his robes revealing the Astronomical egg. He held the alien egg in his possession up over his head as the colosseum cheered. Manzh was more surprised by the crowd's reaction than by the egg reveal. He had no idea the power the egg presented. Code Silver looked into the sky to see himself projected onto the golden dome above. He watched on the screen as General Gold continued to wave around the prize. The General stopped when he stood before Emperor Yujen's royal skybox. Dropping to kneel, General Gold held the egg over his head toward the Emperor. The colosseum fell silent. Manzh stared at the General kneeling across the table from him.

"Emperor Yujen, our most peaceful ruler. I come before you today as you initiate Pax Armata, and I bring a gift," General Gold declared. He did not look up or flinch from his position.

There was thunderous applause as they awaited the Emperor's response.

"What have you brought me today, my Golden friend?" Emperor Yujen asked. The Emperor's skybox sat above the rest, for the Emperor had an order not to be seen. There were rumors within the Seven Colonies about the Emperor, and why he was so reclusive.

"I bring a recent discovery, an ancient evil, for you to make your peace," General Gold announced. The Promethean leader looked up in the Emperor's direction and continued, "This is for you. This is the egg of an Astronomical, and it's your weapon of peace."

The General stood as he raised the egg higher into the air above his head. The crowd continued their thunderous applause.

"General, you may bring me my egg," Emperor Yujen declared as his words garnered more applause.

Before the General could move a voice cried out, "Not so fast." The General turned to find who had interrupted the ceremony. Manzh glanced around as well, as he had considered interrupting at the same moment.

"Who dares speak and interrupt my moment?" Emperor Yujen demanded. His voice was not angry but his shouts echoed through the colosseum.

"I did your grace," A female said as she stood from the Aurelian skybox. She was decorated with necklaces carved from wood and had dark robes underneath. She stared up towards her Emperor as the people with her stood to support her.

"Aurelia, is that you?" Emperor Yujen challenged from the comfort of his skybox above. The Emperor laughed until he choked as the colosseum joined him. The Seven Colonies had grown to resent the Aurelians for their claims to the throne in recent years.

"You know my son's claim to the throne, Yujen, and yet you steal his birthright for your own gain," Aurelia shouted back. Her people nodded along with her. "Now," She continued to shout, "Now you claim this egg that my Son's prophecy warned us of. The egg will not bring peace. You will not bring peace." The woman's screams silenced the Colosseum.

General Gold lowered the egg to relax his arms as he waited for the Emperor's response.

"Aurelia, I have been kind to allow you and your bastard to hang around all these years," Yujen replied. "Now it would appear that your twisted world ideas have found more followers in Aurelius. Am I correct to believe that your Colony doubts my rule?" Emperor Yujen questioned. The people of the Aurelius Colony rallied behind Aurelia.

"I am here to ask your Senate to elect themselves the authority to call off your peace treaty," Aurelia stated. There were cries from the other skyboxes as the opposition made themselves heard.

Emperor Yujen allowed his followers to voice their support for him.

"If my Senate wishes to humor you, I'll allow it," Emperor Yujen laughed. Yujen's supporters broke out in cheers that echoed throughout the Colosseum.

The skybox for the Augustus Colony rose to the level of the Aurelian platform. The Senator from Augustus stood from her seat, with the help of her aid beside her. the two walked to the front of the platform to address Aurelia and the Emperor.

"My Lord, as Senate Leader, I refuse to hear this woman's claims any longer," the Augustan Senator spoke.

"That said," She continued, turning to Aurelia in her skybox. "If it were up to me tonight, I would place Aurelia and her treasonous followers under custody. She has conspired against you for years, and still, she opposes the prospect of peace," The Senator said.

Emperor Yujen's voice called down to give his judgment, "Very well. Aurelia, there you have it. As emperor of the Nomical Order, leader of the Seven Colonies of Man. I hereby place you and your kin with you tonight under arrest." Emperor's decision was met with a mixed reaction of cheers and boos.

"My philosophers are here with me," Aurelia shouted, "They're not here to fight, but they won't allow my arrest. If you make one move towards me, my warriors will do what they must to ensure I leave here." The men around Aurelia all bowed to her. Their dark armor plating underneath their robes covered them head to toe.

Emperor Yujen broke out into laughter again and quickly choked himself up.

"I am declaring peace tonight, and you come for my throne," Emperor Yujen said as he coughed. The Nomical Order's elites awaited the Emperor's next words.

"General Gold," Yujen shouted, "Do you still have my egg?" The voice echoed down to the General who lifted the egg back into the air. "I have it, my lord," Gold declared. The crowd burst back into cheers to the General's delight.

"Right, here's what's going to happen next," Yujen called out, "I'm going to send my emissary to your box to collect the egg. You can trust him." General Gold nodded as he lowered the egg. Suddenly a tall cloaked figure teleported in front of the General. His hood covered his head and whatever else he had underneath it. Out of the shadows of his hood, his pointed chin was visible with fanged teeth exposed.

"Give me the egg," The sturdy figure said with a hand reaching out. His sleeve fell back to reveal sharp fingernails that were clawlike.

Despite his intimidating appearance the General did as his Emperor instructed. The egg was much smaller in the emissary's hands. The cloaked figure's demeanor changed when he held the egg and inspected it.

"Now, General Gold," Emperor Yujen announced.

"I want you to personally see to it that Aurelia and her guests do not leave my palace tonight," Yujen ordered. General Gold nodded and turned his focus on the Aurelian skybox.

"You can make all the order that you want," Aurelia shouted, "But my son will be Emperor. You will not wrong the Nomical Order. To everyone here, my fellow queens and kings, you're about to be the Six Colonies of Man thanks to Emperor Yujen. Blame me all you want, but your Emperor has pulled the veil over your eyes. You're all here tonight to celebrate the destruction of the Seventh Colony. " The crowd burst into an uproar as Aurelia's warning caused alarm.

"Does this mean the rumors are true, Your Grace?" Someone shouted from the Pius Colony.

"Of course they're true, you twit," A senator from the Hadrian Colony replied through the shouts.

"I came here to talk about speculations that the Sunriza may have returned," A Vespasian King cried. He slammed his hairy fist down on the table beside him.

"Do you all see?" Aurelia called out to the masses, "He can't bring you peace."

The Emperor's choking laughter rang out again as he cried out to the General, "Finish them!"

General Gold leaped up into the air like a golden missile headed toward the Aurelians. As the sparkling bomb of a Promethean flew through the air the skyboxes around them lowered.

The Emperor made sure that the rest of his guests would not see the outcome as Gold crashed into the Aurelians. The impact he made caused a splash of gold that showered over his targets. The Aurelians caught in the

General's attack melted to the floor in the pools of gold at their feet. They were pulled across the ground to the reforming body of General Gold. He had grown an extra arm to grab his victims. He held the three Aurelians by their necks as he continued his assault. The General's three arms tossed the limp bodies at the remaining Philosophers. With all his enemies down Gold found Aurelia. She was injured from his divebomb and tried to crawl away on the floor.

"It's no use," Aurelia said as she struggled to catch her breath.

"You can kill me, but my son will be safe, out there," Aurelia gasped as she said her final words.

Gold's third arm launched from his chest. Aurelia smiled as Gold's attack exploded in another golden burst around her.

General Gold turned his back before the impact to avoid watching Aurelia's death. As the smoke settled a silhouette emerged.

"Wait a minute!" Manzh called out. The Emperor laughed from high above the Prometheans. The Silver Promethean took another step closer to General Gold. This is it, Manzh thought.

"What do you want?" Gold asked his subordinate. Code Silver continued to approach his leader one step at a time.

"I want what any second in command wants. To be number one," Manzh stated. "That is why, I'm upholding my code As Silver of the Prometheans and challenging you for the rank of Gold. Right now! Before our Emperor," Manzh spoke with a determination that drove him to take another step.

General Gold chuckled and then looked up toward their Emperor. "What do you say, your Grace?" Gold asked.

The Emperor coughed from above, then called down, "I'll allow it."

General Gold chuckled again as Manzh was suddenly in his face delivering a punch to his dome. Gold's helmet shifted to the right as the punch staggered him back.

"And now he strikes against his true enemy," Gold remarked with another laugh. Manzh cocked back his fist and prepared for another punch. As he swung down towards Gold a part of Gold protruded from his stomach shapeshifting to stab Silver.

The gold piercing through Silver grew more spikes along its length. These extra spikes cut deeper into Silver as he cried out. The gold inside Manzh mutated into an arm of the General. He lifted Manzh into the air before whipping him down to the ground.

"You already healed from my last attack?" General Gold taunted. Code Silver stood from the ground with an exposed area in his armor where he'd been stabbed.

General Gold raised his hands and extended his fingers out toward Code Silver who charged at him. Beads of gold began to form at the General's shoulders and trickle down to his hands. As they reached his fingertips the golden beads propelled like bullets through Manzh. The Silver Promethean struggled to step through the onslaught of gold coming his way. He held his forearms up to shield himself until he had nothing left below his elbows. The gold continued to cut through him as he lowered his arms to heal his hands. The General increased his barrage and even grew another third arm to hold back Manzh but he kept coming. Finally within reach to grab the General, Manzh reflected on everyone he was doing this for. His mother, who he had not seen since he began his code as a Promethean. His father, who had died building the very walls he was standing in. Manzh wrapped his hands around the General's wrists. Beads of gold crawled over his fingers as if they were alive. Manzh cocked back his head to headbutt the General.

I'm even doing this for you, Lo, even though you broke your oath, there's still hope for you, Manzh thought.

His helmet and his skull shattered as he slammed into the General's helmet. *Maybe you can be my Code Silver again, Lo,* Manzh continued to think. His mind healed before their

impact was over. Gold dust rained down around them as Manzh held the headless body of General Gold. The attack had shattered everything above the General's shoulders.

The Emperor began to cheer from his skybox above them.

"Look's like he's been retired," Emperor Yujen commented.

Manzh felt something was off as he looked into the hollow husk of Gold's body. The General's wrists were still in Manzh's hands as they twisted to grab their Silver captor.

"He's hollow!" Manzh called out as the General's shoulder's opened up and his arms pulled Manzh in. General Gold stood to his feet as Code Silver's legs kicked to get free. His torso was inside Gold's shell and he could feel himself being constricted. Manzh punched and squirmed his body but it only pulled him into the golden prison more. Feeling that he was fully submerged Manzh stretched out his arms and legs to try and get free.

The gold around him broke through his silver helmet and filled his visor. Manzh felt the gold enter his body through his nose and mouth. General Gold suffocated Manzh as his golden body disappeared into Code Silver.

The Promethean took a step forward and looked down
at his hand as he swelled up turning into gold. When he was twice his normal size, gold oozed from every one of his pours until General Gold reemerged.

Manzh now stood as a golden statue as the General waited for him to heal and continue fighting. After a minute passed General Gold patted his new statue on the chest and laughed. "He's not coming back from this," He stated.

Emperor Yujen replied, "Yes, well, despite the entertainment, this has ruined my night."

General Gold opened his mouth to apologize but he was cut off by the Emissary. "My Lord, I'm afraid your evening was ruined before it began. This is not the Astronomical Egg that we seek." The cloaked Emissary teleported to the Aurelian skybox where Gold had just fought. He ripped open the egg with his hands and revealed an empty shell.

"What is this?" The Emissary demanded, "Do you think my Master Ammin will be pleased to find out you double-crossed him?"

The Emperor shouted down to the Emissary and PROs below. "What is the meaning of this? You think you can enter my home within my Nomical Order and speak to me in such a way?" The Emperor grew angry as he yelled.

"My Lord," General Gold spoke up, "My Lord, it might be my fault. The unit I sent to retrieve the egg, well, something else happened."

The Emissary turned his attention to Gold standing nearby.

"What? What did he say?" The Emperor called out.

The hooded Emissary asked Gold, "Did your people do something with my egg?" He held up the cracked eggshell. "There's supposed to be a godlike being inside this," The Emissary added.

General Gold nodded and said, "I had a second team that ran recon on the egg and the moon. One of mine went rogue and jeopardized the mission. I've got one here from the unit that can confirm it for ya."

The Emissary grunted and said, "Which one?"

AP felt a lump in his throat form as the General called out for him.

"It's true, she went rogue," AP shouted. He had remained with his fellow Prometheans in their skybox at the table. They were still prisoners after all.

"Let me explain what happened," AP answered. He was astral projecting to the same skybox as Gold and the Emissary. As his projection stood alongside the Emissary he explained what had happened to Red and the egg.

"That would explain it," The Emissary said as he rubbed his chin again. "When your rogue Promethean cracked the egg it fractured reality. What you saw happen during your spirit walk was the true reality," The alien revealed.

"Has this happened before?" AP questioned. The alien nodded and held up his hand.

"We have seen it five other times since discovering the Astronomicals. So far we know that these galaxy-sized beasts reign across realities as gods. This rogue of yours has taken her first step to join them," The Emissary replied.

"Can we fix this?" Emperor Yujen called out from above, "Tell your Master I still want to build our relationship."

The Emissary looked up over his shoulder to the Emperor's skybox.

"I'm afraid not. Ammin will not be pleased to learn this revelation," The Emissary remarked. "The Dynasty will definitely bear the weight of this fracture," He added.

"Bu-But we can still work out negotiations for peace, right?" Emperor Yujen cried out. He sounded nervous.

The Emissary smirked in the shadows of his hood as he fired back, "Don't count on it! The Nomical Order just put all of reality at risk. This affects every living thing in Crude Space, it's beyond us. Ammin will want you to do more than fix this."

The Emperor lowered his skybox slowly. When it was at the same level as the Aurelian skybox it came to a sudden stop. Emperor Yujen walked forward out of the shadows of his skybox. His old physique was highlighted by wrinkles along his dark tan skin. His long braided orange hair was fading to white at the roots.

"I stand before you, Ammin's Emissary, to ask that we be given the time to figure this out," Yujen pleaded. His old face was sincere.

AP never imagined he would have the opportunity to be so close to him. He looked over to the alien Emissary to gauge his reaction.

"Time won't save you from Ammin," The Emissary replied, "It will only delay what he'll have in store for you."

Emperor Yujen laughed in the Emissary's face, coughing up spit as he cackled.

"You think that you can laugh at Ammin?" The Emissary screamed as the insult drove him to action. The alien lunged toward Yujen with his arms held high but he was blocked by a wall of gold.

"You! Take the Emperor and run," General Gold shouted over to AP beside him.

Did he forget I'm a projection, AP thought as Gold continued to hold back the alien.

"Prometheans, get up here and fight for your Emperor!" General Gold shouted to the unit below. The seven jumped into the air. AP ran over to Emperor Yujen and asked him to place his hands out in front of him. As AP grabbed the Emperor's palms he focused on switching places with him.

I hope this works, AP thought as he felt the air around him change. When he opened his eyes AP saw that his physical body had taken the place of Yujen's. He looked over the skybox wall to see Yujen confused below.

As the seven Prometheans descended on the Emissary the Code Black from that unit saw a chance to escape. She used her ability to teleport toward the edge of the colosseum where she could see Olymzes below.

"Not so fast," General Gold shouted, extending an arm out at Code Black along the edge. She levitated into the air as her helmet pulled her back towards the rest of them. General Gold crushed the helmet around her head as she crashed into the ground.

There's gold in our helmets? AP thought to himself.

He used his astral projection again to travel into the upper atmosphere, to the Revan-V.

AUGUSTUS COLONY
Olymzes, Octavian
Revan-V

"Kiwa," AP called out as his projection materialized in the cockpit of the Revan-V.

His Code Green sat ahead of him in her pilot's chair. She jumped in her seat before turning around to greet him.

"Are you ready for us?" She asked her fellow officer. The ship was resting at an idle.

AP shook his head no, and said, "No, I appreciate your willingness to go Kamikaze on the commemoration. But the Emperor's plans fell apart."

Kiwa was relieved and asked, "Does this mean you're coming home too?" She didn't like how AP hesitated to answer her question. Every Promethean knew their retirement came with a visit to the Emperor. General Gold's nickname back on Promethean was the Golden Reaper because he led so many to their fate.

"No, probably not, best thing I can do is give you information before I die," AP replied.

Kiwa fought back her urge to cry as she transcribed AP's final message. The hardest part was knowing that she couldn't give him a hug goodbye in his astral form.

She thought about his brother, the previous Code Black. Ever since she lost him at the hands of Code Red, Kiwa had been ready to die. The only things she had left were AP and her dreams of becoming a WorldPilot.

Losing him was a lot to process knowing that she wouldn't be going with him. As they finished his message and prepared to say goodbye she thought about what she would do after. He was giving her a new reason to live and a new purpose. She found a new resolve to carry on their legacy, for AP and Brek, two brothers who she loved dearly.

AUGUSTUS COLONY

Olymzes, Octavian
Emperor Yujen's Palace
- Royal Colosseum Guest Hall

    As AP snuck away for a moment the other Prometheans carried out their attack on the Emissary. Code White took a barrage of punches and claws but kept coming back for more. Code Red's hypnotism couldn't take control of the Emissary no matter how much they tried. Code Pink was tossed aside into Code Blue. Code Yellow and Green teamed up to fly through the air. Yellow's ability was amplified by Green's giving them full flight. As they soared down through the sky above the Emissary he turned to catch them both. Yellow's spine snapped with whiplash as the alien stopped them in midair with his catch. General Gold fired his bullet's from a distance but the Emissary used the PROs in his hands as shields.
    The alien raised a hand to General Gold as a wave of vibrations cascaded from his palm and engulfed Gold. The leader of the PROs fell to the ground immobilized. The five remaining Prometheans from the CIVth unit stood their ground. They had broken bones from the kicks and punches the alien threw at them.

As they charged the Emissary again he held out both his hands, stating, "I'm bored."

The vibrations from his hands ripped the Promethean's helmets and armor away. The wave continued to vibrate the Prometheans into one another. Even their fallen allies were collected by the attack. The vibrations continued to tear at the seven of them as they fused together into one hideous figure. Their heads were not limited to their shoulders as they had a head for a hand and foot, as well as a head instead of a hip bone. One of their heads on their necks had a foot where the nose once was. The CIVth unit screamed out in pain, as Yellow's broken spine struggled to keep them standing.

General Gold sat up from the floor where he had been knocked unconscious. AP returned to his body to see the disfigurement.

The fused Promethean took a step as it screamed and cried out. It appeared to have a hand trapped under the skin of its chest that wanted out.

The Emissary laughed at his creation. "My Master would love this. I've got an idea," The alien said, "You let me leave and take my art project home to my Master. I'll make sure that he grants the Nomical Order more time to make things right."

General Gold wiped dirt away from his visor.

"How do we know we can trust you?" The General asked.

The Emissary smiled as he relaxed, and said, "You have no choice. I'm not even one of the strongest among my people, but you guys are the best of yours. I'll even let you keep that Abysmal Pontopiddan, so you can hunt more eggs for us. Let's say we reconvene in a year. Yeah?" The Emissary asked.

The skybox where AP had left the Emperor began to rise up to their level. Emperor Yujen stood at the top of it with his arms opened wide.

"Great idea," Yujen called out.

The Emissary adjusted his cloak, and said, "Okay. I'll deliver the news to Ammin. He won't be pleased but he won't order all of our deaths either." The alien collected the deformed Promethean and threw the body over his shoulder.

"Go and tell your Master that the Nomical Order looks forward to joining the Ammin Dynasty," Yujen said. The Emissary nodded and teleported away.

AP was alone with General Gold and the Emperor of the Nomical Order.

"What's the next move?" General Gold asked his Emperor. Yujen turned his back on them and walked to the edge of the skybox to observe the damage to his colosseum.

"Aurelia is no longer an issue but her son is still out there. Pax Armata will have to be delayed until we can figure out what to do about the Dynasty. In the meantime," Yujen commented, "It would be best that you get your PROs in order. Your numbers are dwindling, and I didn't get to add anyone to my trophy collection as promised."

AP knew he was there to die for the Emperor's personal enjoyment, he just wasn't sure how it would happen. He swallowed the lump in his throat as Yujen turned to point at him.

"What does he do?" The Emperor questioned. AP looked to his General that held his fate in his golden hands.

"He's important to me," General Gold said in a low voice. The General didn't look over at AP but if he had he would have been able to see the Promethean's posture change in relief.

Emperor Yujen scoffed and looked AP, Code Black, up and down.

"What's he to you?" The Emperor inquired, still staring at Code Black.

The General lifted his palm into the air as he spoke.

"This one is the key to the moon, Pontoppidan, they're connected," The General said. He turned toward AP and closed his palm making a fist. "Also, he's going to come back with me to Promethean to compete for the Silver Sanction. I may have found my next Code Silver," The General declared.

The Emperor smiled and nodded. "Very well," The Emperor said, "Not a word about what happened here tonight is to leave my Palace. The Seven Colonies need not worry about these things."

General Gold nodded and then bowed to the Emperor. AP did the same out of respect and fear.

"One more thing General," The Emperor added. He turned to General Gold and whispered, "I have another mission for you once you're done on Promethean. I want you to travel to Aurelius and eliminate-"

AP tried his best to hear what the Emperor was whispering but it was unclear. He worried about Kiwa, Code Green, out there alone, delivering AP's warning to the Aurelians.

XII AUGUSTUS COLONY
Promethean
Code Yellow and Code Pink

A dark shadow loomed over the manmade homeworld of the Prometheans. The PROs that captured Pontopiddan delivered the Abysmal moon creature to their homeworld. Pontoppidan orbited the traveling planet through the Augustus Colony awaiting the General's return.

Code Yellow and Pink from the CVIIth unit walked together through the Golden Capital. They returned together after their previous mission to capture Pontoppidan went awry.

Avi, Code Yellow, glanced up every few steps to admire the moon overhead. The thought of being the one to capture the moon excited him when they first took on the task. He was disappointed to learn their mission was over before it really began. Code Pink nudged his arm as Avi continued to watch the moon, reflecting on Code Red's arrest.

"Are you still thinking about Elma?" Code Pink asked his fellow Promethean. Avi turned to his friend as they continued down their path, and replied, "Is it obvious?"

The two PROs passed a group of cadets in the street. The aspiring psychics were still in their academy uniforms despite the late hour. Code Pink waited until they had passed the others before he continued.

"I don't need telepathy to know she's on your mind again," Apax, Code Pink, remarked. Code Yellow sighed as they continued toward the Promethean Library.

"We were partners," Avi groaned, "The three of us had a plan but she stabbed us in the back. Code Black even said she killed us first in his vision." The yellow Promethean's voice grew as his anger returned to him. Code Pink reached out and grabbed Yellow's hand, lowering it.

"Lower your voice, Avi," Code Pink demanded. The two stopped to look around. as they faced each other Code Pink leaned in toward his partner and said, "Let it go. She got caught by Code Black. She's in prison right now while we're free." Code Yellow stared back at his fellow Promethean, wishing he could see behind the mask. He wanted to know what Pink was thinking because he knew that his own emotions were keeping him awake at night. Had Code Black not interfered they would be dead and the forgotten accomplices of Red's plan.

"I still can't figure out why Elma didn't rat us out when they arrested her," Avi said in a lower voice. Pink shrugged as the two continued toward the library.

"She probably didn't want to share the credit," Code Pink commented. The two PROs reached the base of the staircase leading up to the Library of Promethean. At the top of the stairs stood a golden statue of a woman with her hand extended out in front of her face. It depicted the First Promethean who built their homeworld. As the two PROs reached the top they stopped to bow to the statue, as all Prometheans did. The statue appeared sometime in Avi's academic years before he adopted the code. He had heard rumors that the statue was a disobedient student that the General Punished.

"Do you think Code Black and that other unit have made it to the Emperor yet?" Avi whispered. The interior of the library was dark with vast hallways of scrolls and books along the walls. Code Pink trailed behind Code Yellow as they found the section they needed.

"Not yet, we would've gotten word about Pax Armata," Pink replied, "Should be happening soon, though." The pink Promethean grabbed a book and flipped the pages.

Avi looked through the collection of books in front of him as he thought about Code Black. Prometheans knew going to the Royal Palace meant their Code was over.

Code Pink grabbed a stack of books and scrolls and tucked them under his arm. Avi struggled to find anything of interest in the section they were in.

"Avi, come on, pay attention, would ya," Apax whispered. The pink Promethean stepped closer to Code Yellow and handed him a scroll.

"It was your idea to come here and study the Astronomicals," Apax added. The yellow Promethean looked down in the dim light at the scroll in his hands. He brought his pink friend with him in the hopes of learning more about the egg and Pontoppidan.

"I know," Avi replied. He handed the scroll back to Code Pink.

"I think you should be the one to study the Astronomicals," Code Yellow stated. Code Pink took the scroll and tucked it under his arm with the rest.

"Why do I have to be the only one to do it?" Code Pink questioned his friend. Code Yellow motioned for Apax to follow him.

"Because I want to study for something else," Avi whispered as they walked to another wall of books.

Code Pink stared at the titles on the shelf as Avi picked one out.

"Ah," Apax remarked, "So you're going to try your hand at commanding?" Avi picked out a book and nodded.

"I think PROTO Yellow has a nice ring to it," Code Pink laughed. He patted Avi on his back.

Avi laughed and then added, "Code Black gave us a second chance, we owe it to him."

As the two Prometheans checked out of the Library they stepped out into the cold night air. Pontoppidan still lingered in the artificial clouds above them. The two bowed to the statue in front of the Library and descended the stairs. There was a boom that echoed down the golden streets around them as a ship entered the atmosphere.

"I wasn't expecting him back so soon," Code Pink commented. The ship crossed over their heads as the two watched it pass. General Gold's ship had returned from Octavian, along with AP, Code Black.

CLAUDIUS COLONY
Dwarf Star - Estrella
Code Blue and Code White

    The Flat Planet known as the Sunviza shrouded the sky as it cast its long perpetual shadow on the world below. Shortly after arriving in the sky, a small shuttle descended down from the alien planet above.
    The Uzalech villagers wasted no time preparing for the threat heading their way. Lo and Ciela had no other choice but to stay and help the local inhabitants of their new home. The two donned their Promethean armor for the first time since they took their leave. Ciela hugged her partner as they shared a kiss. Lo kept his eyes closed as the kiss ended and placed his white helmet over his head. Ciela looked at her reflection in his visor as she did the same. Code Blue grabbed their dischargers and fastened hers over her shoulder. The heavy strap on the plasma weapon nestled her armored chest.
    She extended the other weapon to Code White, who looked at it and refused.
    "If this comes to a fight, I'll use my hands," Lo replied. The white Promethean turned and headed to the door as Ciela followed. She figured she would bring his discharger with her just in case she needed it.

Outside their home, they were greeted by Senk, Garude, and the other warriors from the village. To Lo and Ciela's surprise, Garude was able to fly in his beast form. They followed Garude on their toars tracking the ship descending from the Sunviza.

When the shuttle landed, a small party of aliens emerged from a hatch with a ramp that extended down to the ground. The four humanoid lifeforms wasted no time exiting their ship. The two leading the way down the ramp pointed their weapons around as they surveyed the area. Their bodies were mechanical and clunky as they moved around like puppets.

When they reached the surface they gave the go-ahead to their Lords behind them to proceed.

A young alien woman stepped between her two guards and removed her hood to reveal glowing skin and eyes. Her freckled face sparkled in the night. The rest of her features were humanlike, including her long white hair she kept tied back behind her head.

A much slower figure at the back of the pack walked with a cane that wobbled as it supported him along each step. He emitted the same glow from his body as the younger woman accompanying him.

"There's something approaching, Milady," One of the guards commented. His metallic skin reflected the light from his superiors. There was a cry coming from the trees nearby that intensified as more voices joined in.

"Do you hear that?" The elder man perked up as he asked. His hunched back stood a little straighter as his grip on his cane tightened. The metallic guards aimed their weapons at the tree line in the distance.

"Fucking birdcalls," The young woman called out. Her voice sounded both pleased and annoyed as she licked her lips.

Senk led the villagers out of the trees as their toars sprinted toward the foreign ship. The Uzalech broke off into two groups forming a perimeter around their guests. They continued to cry out as they waved their winged arms over their heads. They brandished their wooden hunting spears as they waved them in the air.

Garude flew down through the air and landed several feet from the invaders. The membranes of his wings retracted into his arms as he stood. The glowing woman held up an arm in disgust to defend herself. Her two guards stepped in the middle of them with their weapons drawn. Garude hissed at them, exposing his teeth and extending his talons further.

"You must be the Werephoenix," The Woman stated from behind her guards. Garude had a menacing appearance but the woman still had about a foot in height on him. Her guards were almost twice his size but Garude stood his ground.

"That's right," Garude hissed. The warriors from his village cheered him on from behind.

"Do you know who I am?" The Woman questioned. Her men chuckled as they kept their aim on Garude.

Garude's hiss turned into a growl. He didn't speak as he stared into the face of the glowing woman before him. He had a good idea of who she was based on her looks.

"I'm the Sunriza," She declared, "You killed someone very dear to me." Garude was surprised to hear this news. He thought he had killed the Sunriza already.

"How can you be the Sunriza?" Garude barked, "He's dead." The Uzalech all cheered again behind Garude.

The Sunriza's expression grew angry, "That was my predecessor," She said. "You see my Gramps behind me? He's the first Sunriza," She added. Her grandfather behind her stepped forward and licked his lips to speak.

"You killed my legacy, child," The elder Sunriza complained. He looked at his armed guards with their weapons ready and then held up his hand.

"Guards," The Elder ordered, "Shoot that one." The Guards looked to see the Sunriza pointing in Senk's direction in the crowd.

Garude turned to his cousin and wanted to tell him to run. His next thought was to jump in and attack the guard but he froze.

Two shots rang out only they came from the trees behind them. The first shot missed but the second hit its mark, taking out the guard aimed at Senk.

The second Guard tried to return fire at Code Blue in the trees but Code White materialized in front of him. The Promethean noticed the first guard on the ground was made of tech. Code White phased his hand into the chest plate of the remaining Guard and removed its glowing core. The Guard's eyes faded as it fell to its knees and collapsed over.

Garude ran to Senk as everything happened, leaving Lo face-to-face with the Sunriza. The white Promethean dropped the core from his hand and raised his fists in a defensive stance.

"You made a mistake coming here," Code White said.

The young Sunriza smirked, and replied, "You're the one that just made a mistake." She raised her hand and extended her palm toward the Promethean.

"I'm a Promethean from the Nomical Order," Code White explained. "We bought this planet through an auction house on StarMetro. I'm going to have to ask you to stop threatening my people and get off my planet," He added. The woman standing before him didn't seem too pleased.

"Humans have been stealing from us for centuries," The Woman replied. Her hand still aimed at Code White as it began to charge an orb of light. "You may have bought this rock, but we own the star you see in the sky," She added.

"No!" Code Blue cried out from the trees as she fired another shot.

She missed again, hitting the dirt several inches from the young Sunriza's feet.

The glowing alien smirked again at Code White in front of her, then redirected her aim at the trees. She fired a flash of light that struck Code Blue's tree and set it on fire.

Code White turned to the Uzalech behind him and ordered them to retreat. Everyone but Garude did as they were instructed.

Code White turned back to the Sunriza standing in front of him and readied his fist. His punch flew through the air but landed in the palm of the elder Sunriza. He moved so fast Lo never saw him step in between him and the other Sunriza. The older figure no longer held his cane and his shakes were gone. His grip held onto Code White no matter how much he tried to get out of it.

"Its no use," The Sunriza laughed. His body cracked as his muscled expanded and his back straightened out. "My name is Zol, and I am the light," He added.

"Reya, take care of the other one," The elder Sunriza yelled out. His granddaughter nodded and leaped toward the trees. Garude charged at Zol but the Sunriza deflected him away with a ray of light from his free hand.

The glowing alien lifted Lo into the air so that they could be eye to eye and growled, "You can't run from the light."

XIII AUGUSTUS COLONY
Promethean Tournament Grounds
Code Black

Promethean tradition dictated that a battle royale would be held to select a new Code Silver. Each unit elected one of their own members to participate in the challenge. Despite the elections, it was customary for the PROTO member of the unit to compete.

AP found himself thrown into the competition with no choice. He didn't imagine he would survive this long, let alone have this opportunity. He knew he had to do this for his brother, and for everyone in his Colony back home.

When he arrived on Promethean with General Gold he was taken to the Tournament Grounds. Word had spread of the Silver Sanction and challengers had already been selected. The five other PRO's elected to compete stood in the arena with General Gold.

AP couldn't believe that the General he had travelled with was not the real one, but a golden clone. The clone merged into the original as he greeted AP.

"The six of you are about to compete for the Silver Sanction," General Gold declared. He held a silver sash in his hands and showed it to the group of competitors.

"Remember, the rules are to incapacitate your opponents, not kill," The General instructed.

The leader of the Prometheans used his ability to raise the floor below them up into the arena above. As the ceiling opened up for them the crowd of Promethean spectators outside cheered.

General Gold greeted the crowd and gave them the same rundown of the rules before leaving for his seat. A golden throne sat above the crowd with a clear view of the tournament grounds below.

"Give us a good show," The General called out from his throne, "And let the Silver Sanction commence!"

The crowd was in an uproar as the combatants stood together in the open arena.

Code Black stood still among his competition and watched the crowd cheer. The fight had been over before it began. The five other PROs stood frozen, petrified in the astral plane where Code Black had lured them. It happened the moment the ceiling opened on the platform.

He used his ability and turned the ceiling opening into a portal to the astral plane.

The other PROs were trapped as soon as General Gold brought them into the arena.

The crowd's cheers turned to boos as Code Black and his fellow PROs remained immobile in the arena. General Gold shifted in his seat as he waited for someone to move.

AP turned to the General and bowed, as the crowd fell silent. Their confusion transitioned to cheers as they realized the battle royale was over. AP, Code Black, had won the title of Code Silver.

AUGUSTUS COLONY
Code Yellow

Avi was surprised to learn that Code Black had returned from the Emperor's palace. After the Silver Sanction he found AP, now Code Silver, and congratulated his squad mate. As the two reunited they were surprised to see Code Green had returned to Promethean as well. She ran to AP in his fresh silver attire and jumped into his arms. Avi smiled under his yellow visor as he watched the two embrace.
"I didn't think you were going to make it," Kiwa, Code Green, said as she hugged her friend.
"I can't believe I'm still here," AP replied. His helmet shined brightly as the two pulled away from each other.
"I did exactly as you said," Kiwa commented. "I just got back and heard the news," She added.
AP smiled inside his silver helmet. He was relieved to hear that Kiwa had delivered his message for him.
As the three continued to catch up Code Pink came running up to them.
"There you are," The pink Promethean shouted. He hugged Code Green and patted AP's back to congratulate him as Code Silver.
"Were you looking for us?" AP asked as Code Pink pulled his hand from AP's shoulder.

"I'm surprised you don't know already," Code Pink replied.

AP stared back at his subordinate and wondered what he was talking about.

"We were just given an assignment, I had to deal with Topaz Jack by the way," Code Pink said the last part with a groan.

"What is it?" Code Green chimed in. She looked over to Code Silver to admire his new look one more time.

"Get this," Code Pink laughed, "We're going back to Pius to pick up a new Code Black."

Avi laughed and commented, "Better to go there then all the way to Aurelius." The yellow Promethean laughed then added, "Sorry, Silver," as he looked at AP.

AP looked at his unit then smiled and said, "Okay, then we'd better contact Code Blue and Code White for the mission."

CLAUDIUS COLONY
Dwarf Planet - Estrella

Code White struggled as he gasped for air. He had to ration his breaths because the oxygen was low where he was. The Promethean sighed as he began to count down the seconds until he could breathe again. After his defeat in battle against the Sunriza, Lo had been imprisoned in a light beam. The Promethean was unsure of Code Blue and the Uzalech's fate outside the prison.

Another one of his visions appeared to him as they often did. His hallucination showed him Code Red back on Pontoppidan, a place Lo had never gone. He watched as another version of himself fought the growing power of Code Red. She laughed as she opened a portal to an unfamiliar world and pushed the other Code White inside. As the Red Promethean looked at her hand to grasp the power she possessed she turned to her onlooker, Lo.

"You," The Red Promethean shouted, "I will get out of this illusion."

"Do you hear me!" She cried out again, lunging for Lo. The light beam encasing him faded to white as the Promethean floated in the void.

Lo thought about Ciela and what Code Black had warned him about during their last mission. Then he thought about his time as Code Silver and what happened to the General's daughter.

Suddenly Code Silver stood before him in the light. Code White closed his eyes, too afraid to look at the reflection of his mistakes.

A familiar voice called out to him, "Code White, it's me," The voice echoed, "I can't believe I finally found you."

Lo opened his eyes and took another look at the Code Silver standing before him.

"Manzh?" Lo called out. He didn't see Manzh's yellow highlights accenting his armor. This version was different. This Code Silver had purple highlights, signifying his Aurelian roots. Lo realized it was Code Black from his unit and reached out a hand.

The two were able to connect with each other despite Lo being intangible and Silver's astral form.

"Where are you?" AP questioned. Lo explained what had happened with the Sunriza and how to find their planet.

Code Silver nodded along and then said, "I'm going to need you with me for what I'm about to do. If I get you out of here can I count on you to help me?"

Lo thought about it for a moment as he stared into AP's silver visor.

"What choice do I have?" The white Promethean said as he looked around at his hardlight prison, "What do you need me to do?"

AP reached out his hand as he made his offer, "I'll come and help you," He said, "If you help me stop General Gold."

ZANE PALMER

End of Crude Space
Part II

CRUDE SPACE: SILVER SANCTION

ZANE PALMER

CRUDE BRONZE SPACE

CRUDE SPACE: BRONZE

INTRO

Time is of the essence as Pax Armata remains in limbo. The Nomical Order has begun questioning Emperor Yujen's leadership as rumors spread. *The Seven Colonies of Man* fear they may soon be at war with one another once more.

Deep within the Claudius Colony, Code Silver leads a team of *Prometheans* in an effort to save his allies. There they find themselves face to face with two sun gods in an assault that will be known as the 'Battle of Ash and Stars.'

On the other side of the galaxy, a pair of PROs carry out their quiet mission alone aboard the Hyper-Train. Unfortunately for them, an unexpected guest makes himself known.

CRUDE SPACE: BRONZE

XIV PIUS COLONY

Hyper-Train
Code Pink and Code Yellow

The Hyper-Train neared the Galactic Port of Pius as two PROs embarked on their mission. Avi, Code Yellow, had accompanied Apax, Code Pink, on their mission to retrieve the new Code Black. The Senate halted travel to the Aurelius Colony years ago at the Aurelian's own requests. As the two PROs awaited their stop they found themselves in the Trains cantine. The pair were on their second round of malted feeding tubes in the back of the lounge as they went over their plans.

"We grab Code Black and hightail it over to the others," Avi whispered. He leaned over the machines pumping intoxicating stimulants into their veins. His Yellow Promethean helmet reflected his pink teammate in his visor.

Their team was assigned a new Code Black immediately after AP took on the mantle of Code Silver. Avi was happy to go with his friend and confidant Apax, despite feeling like they got a bum deal. He wanted to be with his teammates aboard the Revan-V on their way to liberate Code White and Code Blue.

"You know," Apax replied, "I'm the telepath but what you're saying, sounds like yer reading my mind." The pink Promethean removed his feeding tube and shook it before placing it back in.

"Galactic cheapskates," He added, commenting on the feeding tube's early shut-off. Avi groaned as his connection ended shortly after. "Another round?" Apax suggested, "I'm buyin' again."

The Yellow Promethean declined. "We need to be prepared for when we greet our new teammate," Avi said. He pulled out a dataplate from his bag at his side. The display lit up with text and images of Prometheans.

"You call studying preparing?" Apax remarked. The pink Promethean ordered a third round for himself and sat back to enjoy the rush that came with it.

Avi rolled his eyes in his helmet at his gluttonous friend. "I've asked AP to push my name forward in the PROTO exams," Avi replied. He focused on his dataplate as he scrolled through the material on display. "I want to be ready to lead our team when the time comes," The Yellow PRO added, "This new Code Black will be a part of that unit."

Apax adjusted the cape draped over his shoulders. "I admire your determination," He said, "You got this Avi." The pink Promethean retrieved a dataplate of his own from his bag and tried to turn it on.

"Must need a charge," Apax sighed. He sat the device down on the table and looked through his bag for a charging adapter.

"What have you been studying?" Avi asked. He put his dataplate away after quickly finishing the section he was on.

He admired Avi's speedy reading skills. Apax had brought a series of scrolls from the early days of the PROs from the Promethean Library. The texts were uploaded to his dataplate before their trip but he had only read a few pages.

"Understanding the Clear," Apax remarked, holding up his adapter for his unusable dataplate. He plugged his device into a nearby port and sat it down to charge.

"What is the Clear?" Avi asked.

Before Apax could reply the Hyper-Train's comms speakers fired on. An automated voice alerted all the passengers of their arrival at the Galactic Port of Pius.

As the two PROs made their way to the exit bay they continued their conversation. "The texts say that the Clear is a form of matter produced when an Astronomical dies," Apax whispered.

The pair walked side by side through the crowds waiting to reach the Pius Colony. They made their way toward the front of a large gathering of people at the main gate for departures.

"Is it dangerous?" Avi asked under the echoes of the crowd. The pink PRO beside him stood on his toes to get a better view of the crowd ahead.

"No, it's an energy source," Apax replied, "It provided mankind with unimaginable abilities. I read that the first ones to harness the Clear went on to establish the Promethean Code."

The two Prometheans made it through the exit and into the terminal outside the train. They traveled light with only one bag each. As they moved through the crowd waiting to board the train they found an elevator. Inside the small lift, the two PROs turned their attention to finding Code Black.

"He's supposed to be at the central plaza, near the inspection bays," Avi stated. The two PROs looked at a holo-map on the elevator wall showcasing the different levels. The projection showed that they were five floors below the plaza.

"He should be through with his inspection by now, right?" Apax asked. The elevator ascended the floors toward the central plaza as the two waited for the doors to swing open.

"Think so," Avi replied. The metallic doors slid open as light filled the space around them. Outside the elevator, a large open area with shops and pedestrians filled the floor. The pair of PROs emerged from the elevator into the central plaza of the Galactic Port of Pius.

"There's the inspection bay," Avi commented. The yellow Promethean pushed through the crowd with Apax, Code Pink, close behind.

"I think I see him," Avi called out. "Yeah, I see his helmet, and," he paused, then said, " Apax, don't freak out."

Apax stopped behind his friend and wondered what Avi was warning him about. He looked beyond Code Yellow in front of him to see the new Code Black up ahead. By the inspection bays, a slim man dressed in fresh Promethean attire waited for them. The PRO was not alone as Avi and Apax had anticipated. Instead, he had a familiar figure standing at his side.

"Oh no," Apax sighed, "It's-" Before he could finish his sentence he was cut off.

"Howdy, Howdy," Topaz Jack shouted.

XV CLAUDIUS COLONY
Dwarf Planet Estrella - Sunviza
Revan-V

    The metallic world of the sun gods known as the Sunviza had completed its eclipse of the planet Estrella. On the far side of the globe, the Revan-V entered into orbit, hurdling through its ashy atmosphere. Kiwa, Code Green, piloted her ship carrying a ragtag team of Prometheans. The squad was recruited at the last minute and led by AP, Code Silver. Alongside Kiwa and AP, were Code Red, Code Yellow, and Code Black. The three PROs competed for the Silver Sanction alongside AP, where he recruited them.
    AP, Code Silver, needed to rescue Lo and Ciela if he was going to stop General Golds' attack on Aurelius. Lo, Code White, had survived the General's wrath once before, during his own sanction as Code Silver. AP knew the white Promethean's abilities and knowledge of the General were invaluable.
    As she flew, Kiwa wondered how the mission was going for Code Pink and Yellow from her own unit. She checked her timepad.

They should be on their way back to Promethean aboard the Hyper-Train with Code Black by now, She thought.

"Code Green," AP called out from the seat ahead of her, "Do you see that up ahead?" At the front of the cockpit, AP sat in their former squad leader's seat. The silver PRO pointed ahead as the others behind him mumbled to themselves.

"I see it," Kiwa replied. her green visor lit up from the light reflecting off of the cockpit display. Beyond the metal deserts on the horizon, a towering castle of light illuminated the sky. The glow of the castle flickered and danced like a candle flame as a bolt of light came straight at the Revan-V.

Kiwa maneuvered the ship to avoid the radiant light attack but she wasn't fast enough. The ultralight beam vaporized the Revan-V's left wing mid-barrel roll.

"This wasn't supposed to happen!" AP shouted. He unbuckled his seatbelt and then adjusted the silver sash draped across his chest. He stood from his seat and rushed toward the back of the cockpit, motioning for the others to join him. Code Red, Yellow, and Black followed AP out of the cockpit as Kiwa struggled to steer the ship with only one engine.

The four Prometheans made their way to the exit bay of the Revan-V as Kiwa leveled the ship out. She held back tears as the ship called out to her in agony.

Au-zzz-Auto-zzz-pilot, The Revan-V cried out inside Kiwa's mind. Her connection to the ship amplified the pain back to her physically, numbing her left arm.

"Kiwa, what's your status?" Code Silver called out across the comms.

The green Promethean focused on the source of the light attack in the distance. She was still approaching the metallic structure despite losing altitude.

"I'm here, AP," Kiwa shouted back into the comms, "But listen, without that wing, we're missing half our landing gear. I'm going to take us as close as I can, but you're all gonna have to jump."

Go -zzz- with them, Revan-V pleaded in Kiwa's mind.

"What about you?" AP asked.

Kiwa reflected on everything she had risked since the loss of her Code Black, Brek. She had abandoned her dream of becoming a WorldPilot in favor of reuniting with her lost love. Without landing gear, she had no way to put the Revan-V down safely, and she wasn't going to leave her ship to crash alone.

"I'll get us as close as I can," Kiwa said, "After that, it's up to you." She closed the channel before AP could respond and locked down the exit bay so he couldn't come back for her. After a few moments, she saw that the four other Prometheans had evacuated the ship.

She continued to keep the Revan-V in the sky as they approached the light source ahead. A metallic city lit up as if it were on fire like a beacon shining up to the stars. At the center was a massive castle towering above like a mountain. The castle hovered above the center of a large hole that spanned for miles. The rim waterfalled molten metal down a shaft into the core of the planet Estrella, below. If she couldn't reach the Sunriza's castle to crash, then Kiwa planned to put the Revan-V down in the planet's core.

CLAUDIUS COLONY
Revan-V Exit Bay
Code Silver

As much as it pained him, AP didn't have time to worry about Kiwa's decision to stay aboard the ship. Although AP and Kiwa barely knew each other prior to Brek's death, he had noticed a change in her after their loss.

AP grabbed his drop-pack, lifted the heavy tech to his back, and slid his arms into the shoulder straps. The silver PRO connected the buckle across his chest securing his pack to his body as the others did the same.

"This could get tricky down there, is everyone ready?" AP asked. The three PROs who had opposed him during the Silver Sanction nodded along.

"As long as nobody tries to cheat us," Code Black scoffed from behind the others. The cloaked Promethean was thin and tall, towering over the two PROs in front of him. His crossed arms rested against his armor chest plate.

AP stared up at Code Black through his silver visor. "We were in the arena," AP said, "I was leveling the playing field." He reflected on his decision to pull his opponents into the astral plane to battle for the Sanction. Despite the competition's abrupt end, the PROs in the astral plane fought for weeks for the role.

"Yeah, you said that before," Code Black fired back, "And I'll say it again, when this is over I want a rematch, got it?" The Promethean stretched out his long slim arm toward AP who accepted.

After their fistbump, AP looked at the others and invited them to join the rematch. He had no interest in the role of Code Silver beyond using the position's influence to stop General Gold. He was still haunted by the Golden PRO's rampage against Aurelia in Emperor Yujen's Palace. AP knew once he freed Lo and Ciela they would have limited time to rally more PROs, if any, to oppose the General. He thought about the Emperor's command for General Gold to travel to the Aurelius Colony. The Emperor had something wicked planned for the Aurelians, AP just knew it.

"It's time to jump!" Code Red shouted. The Promethean's voice pulled AP out of his thoughts and back into the exit bay.

"Let's go," AP stated. He shook off his nerves and turned toward the exit doors, activating them. As the Revan-V descended at a low altitude on the outskirts of the city the four PROs jumped from the failing ship.

The air on the Sunviza was full of soot and ash as AP steered through his free fall. He triggered a switch on his drop-pack extending two long metallic legs from the gear on his back. The legs extended out several feet past his own as he fell. Then a tiny compartment on each leg popped open to reveal a mast and a pair of vinyl sail-like wings. The legs kicked through the air guiding AP across the sky above the desert on the outskirts of the city.

AP watched the smoke from the Revan-V fade into the horizon along with Code Green. He hoped that somehow, some way, his friend would escape the ship before it crashed.

The four PROs landed their gliders in a clear area on some dunes beyond the city. Code Red scouted ahead of the others. AP and Code Yellow were close behind with Black on their six. The four regrouped on Red's vantage point overlooking the locale.

"How many do you see?" AP asked. He pulled a scoped discharger rifle from his drop-pack to get a better look. The other PROs did the same with their plasma weapons.

"Far as I can tell," Code Red replied, "Fifty, maybe sixty men, just from counting the huts. Look out yonder east, two armed guards on the entrance to the city. Two more west-side."

AP scanned the perimeter for the guards Red pointed out. The mechanical men carried spears adorned with feathers of various sizes and colors. Their chests emitted a glowing light that traveled down their appendages.

"Dilemen," AP stated, "Code White described them to me when I located him in the astral plane. Code Red, can you do your thing?" AP kept his scoped rifle focused on the two guards stationed to the east.

The Red Promethean stretched his arms and legs to warm up before cracking his knuckles. "Don't blink," The PRO replied. His ability allowed him to shapeshift instantly to resemble anyone he saw. His red helmet shifted to a cold grey as his body morphed to match. He became the spitting image of a Dileman standing before them.

"Woah!" Code Yellow exclaimed. She had seen Code Red shapeshift in the astral plane during the battle royale, but only into another PRO. The transformation from human to machine took Yellow, and the others by surprise.

"Well," Code Red asked, "Do I look good or what?" He turned back and forth to model his mechanical body and sharp fin protruding from his disc, round back.

"You look-" Code Yellow started in but was cut off.

"Where's your light?" AP interrupted, "You don't have the weird chest glow goin' on." He lowered his discharger further, using his free hand to point out the difference in Code Red's form.

Code Black nodded and said, "Ya look ridiculous with or without the glowy chest."

The Red Promethean snapped back, enraged at the comment, "What do you know about glowing? I've only ever seen you lurking in the shadows!" As he lashed out his chest began to glow from his growing frustration.

Code Black eased up upon hearing Code Red's response. His ability to manipulate shadows caused him to walk a fine line between light and dark. He constantly struggled to tip the balance toward the light despite the shadows' hold on him.

"I didn't mean to offend you," Code Black apologized. He had been rude to his unit before and suspected his nomination for the Silver Sanction was to get him off the team.

Code Red scoffed and replied, "Just make sure you've got my back out there, got it?" The Red Promethean disguised as a Dileman waited for a response.

Code Black remained silent and gave a stoic thumbs up. AP sighed as he watched the two finish their back and forth.

"Okay," AP said, "Red, now that you've got the look why don't you head down into the city and see what intel you can gather? Take Code Black with you."

Code Black cracked his knuckles, imitating Code Red from earlier. "Let's do this," he shouted. *Why am I like this?* He thought to himself after. The Promethean dove into the ground at Code Red's feet, disappearing into the PRO's shadow.

XVI GALACTIC PORT OF PIUS

Hyper-Train Boarding Platform Code Yellow and Pink

"I'm gonna have to insist on this one," Topaz Jack said. The rejected Promethean turned informant followed close behind Avi, Apax, and Code Black. The Two PROs hurried along with their new teammate as they rushed through the crowd. The platform to board the Hyper-Train was packed during this galactic time of day.

"No thanks, we already have our tickets booked," Apax fired back, "They're nonrefundable. You know how cheap these guys are." The pink Promethean glanced back at Topaz Jack to see he was still in pursuit.

"Hurry up," Apax said under his breath. The two Prometheans with him nodded and picked up their pace to match Code Pink.

They approached the entry bays to the Hyper-Train where a long line had formed to enter. Apax felt a hand grab his pink shoulder pad and turned to see Topaz Jack had caught up with them.

"Trust me, yer not gonna get to Promethean any faster than you will on my ship, let me take ya," Topaz Jack said. His grip on Pink's shoulder tightened as he spoke. "I'm goin' that way," He added, "Got business over there."

Apax looked over at Avi for backup on talking them out of traveling with Topaz Jack. He wished their helmets didn't block his telepathy so he could speak to his teammate in private.

"No thanks, we're-" Apax began to speak as three cloaked men in front of them turned around draped in Topaz armor. The armored men drew their dischargers and fixed them on the Three PROs.

"I told ya," Topaz Jack sighed, still holding Code Pink's shoulder, "I'm gonna have to insist you come with me on this one."

CLAUDIUS COLONY
Dwarf Planet Estrella
Code Red and Black

"Walk straight!" Code Black cried out. He was tucked away safely in his teammate's shadow dragging across the surface of the world. The distant castle reflected light illuminating the ashy skies beyond the city ahead.

"You think it's easy carrying you on my back like this?" Code Red snapped back. The Promethean disguised as a Dileman panted with each step as he continued on his path.

"Am I that heavy?" Code Black asked. He had never thought about weighing someone down by their shadow before. He preferred using his ability offensively and had trained it for combat purposes.

Code Red shifted to balance himself as he neared the entrance to the city. At the gate two Dilemen stood guard with their feathered spears.

"We're here," Code Red replied, "Act natural."

Code Black did his best to stay still in his shadowy form. *How does a shadow naturally act?* He thought to himself sarcastically.

The two Dilemen standing guard took notice of Code Red approaching them. He stood straight and walked like a human would walk. The two techno-figures looked at each other and then back at the disguised Code Red. The guards began to march toward Red swaying their hunched bodies from side to side as if they were puppets. Code Red took notice of their demeanor and began to match their strides.

"Howdy," Code Red called out. His voice was still human disguised by his Promethean voice modulator.

What are you doing? Code Black thought from the shadows, Don't use galactic slang on these guys. If he still had a physical form he would have his face buried in his palm.

The two guards glanced at each other again, both puzzled by the newcomer's strange ways. They turned back to Code Red and brought their spears across their chest to salute.

"Howdy howdy," The guard on the right replied. The Dileman's voice was robotic with a hint of static feedback at the end of each word.

"Nope, not imitating that one," Code Red mumbled under his breath to Code Black. His ability only allowed him to change his appearance. He couldn't imitate sound or smell the same way he wouldn't be able to fly if he took on a winged form.

"What are you doing outside of the circuit?" The left guard questioned. The Dileman raised his arm and pointed back toward a series of huts behind them. Before Code Red could make up an excuse the guard added, "Get back to your post."

Code Red sighed in relief and then immediately caught himself. Do these things even breathe? He wondered.

"Are you dim, Dileman?" The right guard barked, "Or didya forget yer place in the chain?" As he shouted he slammed the heel of his spear into the metallic soil.

"Actually, I did," Code Red said.

"Oh, so you are dim?" The right guard remarked, "My apologies. Better let me take you to the Medbay." The guard relaxed his grip on his spear and turned to lead Code Red into the city.

"let's go," Code Black whispered.

Code Red began to follow the guard, mimicking the mechanical man's movements. As he followed he turned to the dunes where Code Silver and Yellow were waiting and gave them a shrug. He figured the two PROs were still watching their every move.

The Dileman guard escorted Code Red to a large tent and motioned for him to enter.

"In there," The Dileman said.

Code Red looked back to the dunes one last time before entering the medical tent. Inside he found the room dark and empty.

"Where's the Doc?" Code Red asked.

The Dileman behind him thrust his spear at Code Red, but Code Black emerged from his shadow to catch the blade.

"We don't have a Doctor," The guard declared, "Just an imposter."

The Dileman pulled his spear away from Code Black and threw his foot up into the air, kicking the two PROs to the ground. Code Red clutched his ribs where the kick had landed. He could barely breathe as he propped himself up on his free elbow.

"How-" Code Red asked, "How did you know?" His chest and ribs were on fire as he caught his breath between his words. He looked around for Code Black, who had vanished during the attack.

"We're all connected in this circuit city you wandered into," The Dileman confessed. He raised his mechanical arms over Code Red with his spear aimed at the disguised PRO. As he swung his weapon down at Code Red the Dileman turned it on himself. He lunged the spear through his own torso and then dropped to the ground.

Code Black appeared out of the fallen Dileman's shadow. He had manipulated the mechanical man like a puppet to save Code Red.

"Let's go," Code Black said. He offered Code Red a hand up off the ground. The red Promethean was still disguised and still in pain from his broken ribs. He stumbled over to the real Dileman keeled over on the ground beside them.

"Let's go!" Code Black shouted again. He watched as Code Red removed the Dileman's core from its chest and placed it under his arm.

"I've got an idea on how to distract them," Code Red stated. He patted the core resting under his other arm.

Code Black glanced out the door where he could see more Dileman approaching outside.

As a squad of Dilemen approached the tent Code Red stumbled out holding the core and shouted, "Help! Help! They're in there!" As he pointed back to the tent behind him. Code Black hid within Red's shadow, giving him the support needed to stand.

The Dilemen wasted no time rushing toward the tent with their spears drawn. Code Black crept out of the shadows behind Code Red and moved to one of the Dilemen who passed by. Inside the tent, the Dileman collapsed under the weight of its own shadow as Code Black emerged.

The Promethean's shadowy form reached a second Dileman and contorted its finned spine. The mangled tech fell to the ground as Code Black's onslaught continued on the three others.

He regrouped with Code Red outside, who had already signaled Code Silver and Yellow to join them. The Four regrouped to discuss their next move and to evaluate Code Red's injuries.

"What do we do now?" Code Yellow asked. She used her ability to alter Code Red's perception, blocking him from perceiving any of the pain.

"Whoa, how'd you do that?" Code Red asked. He took several deep breaths as he patted his chest and ribs where the pain had been.

"I didn't do anything," Code Yellow replied, " and stop hitting yourself. I blocked your perception of the pain, but the injury is still real."

The Yellow PRO turned to Code Silver and Black who were keeping a lookout."What's the plan?" Code Yellow asked.

Code Silver turned back to her but before he could respond a flash of light sparked between them. Standing amongst the Prometheans was Reya, one of the two Sunrizas that ruled over the planet. Code Yellow's ability to alter her perception allowed her to react in time. She sidestepped the blue-skinned Sunriza standing before her, who laughed upon seeing Yellow.

"Well, what a surprise," Reya said. The female Sunriza took a moment to look at the four Prometheans. "You must be pretty foolish to come here, child," Reya laughed. She lashed out at Code Yellow with her fist but the Promethean dodged the sun god's strike.

"Interesting," Reya commented, "You're a quick one, well, no matter. These others will do." She turned her attention to Code Silver behind her.

Just as Reya was about to reach AP, Code Yellow used her ability on the silver Promethean. AP avoided the Sunriza's punch at the last second as they moved at rivaled speeds.

"That's enough of that," Reya said, turning her attention back to Yellow. Code Yellow looked over at Code Silver and the others. Before she could say a word Reya was on her again, forcing Code Yellow to run.

AP watched the two race off into the desert as his perception returned to normal. Code Red and Black had no idea what had happened but it didn't matter. Reya had brought an army of Dilemen with her, and they were advancing on the Prometheans.

TRAJAN COLONY
Breachwinde Mid-Drift
Code Yellow and Pink

    Topaz Jack's ship, the Breachwinde, traveled faster than the laws permitted. The Rejected Promethean members of the Topaz squadron hailed from the Seven Colonies. Their customs were similar to the Prometheans. They were dressed in Topaz versions of the PRO's gear.
    Avi and Apax, Code Yellow and Pink respectively, were being entertained in the mess hall. The pair of Prometheans sat together in silence at a round table connected to feeding tubes. There were two Topaz Rejects stationed in the room with them, keeping tabs on the PROs.
    The two PROs had been forced aboard the ship back at the Port of Pius and then treated as guests once they took off. Despite their warm welcome on the ship, Avi noticed the Topaz squad hadn't given them a moment alone.
    Avi focused on his telekinetic abilities. He had to get everything just right. Reaching out with his mind the Yellow Promethean found the panel for the lighting. With a telekinetic thought, Code Yellow shut off the lights, blacking out the room.

The two Rejects didn't suspect a thing from the PROs. The Topaz guards sprang up from their seats in the dark but as soon as they turned their backs the lights were back on. Avi had done everything he needed to do in the one second the lights were out.

In that short time, the Yellow PRO spliced his and Code Pink's feeding tubes together. The Topaz guards shrugged off the lighting issue and returned to their seats.

Avi wanted to communicate with Code Pink, and he had seen Code Green do a similar trick with the Revan-V before.

I hope this works, Avi thought. He began to wonder how he would get Code Pink's attention.

"Avi? Is that you?" Code Pink thought aloud in Code Yellow's head. *"How did you-"* He paused before adding, *"Never mind, I read your thoughts. I can't believe you found a way to bypass the helmets."*

The two PROs continued to sit in silence as they began their telepathic conversation.

"Do you think they know about us?" Avi thought. He recalled their alliance with Code Red, which would have led to their deaths if not for AP, Code Black. He still couldn't accept being Code Red's first victim during the Pontopiddan mission.

Apax's mind focused on comforting thoughts that flooded into Avi's head. *"Nobody knows about that, okay?"* Apax reassured his friend. *"Elma's locked up who knows where, and she has too much pride to admit she wasn't acting alone. I think we're in the clear,"* The pink PRO shared his thoughts.

Avi sighed in relief. *"But if we're not in custody for that then why did they separate us from the new guy, Code Black?"* Avi wondered. He looked around the mess hall and at the two Topaz guards.

"That's a good question," Apax thought back. The pink PRO was excited to demonstrate his abilities more for his friend. *"Hang onto something,"* He added.

Avi gripped his seat with both hands as his mind wandered off. He felt a pull on his neck and spine before disappearing into thought. Apax appeared out of the fleeting images dancing around the room around them.

"What is this?" Code Yellow asked as he looked into a void that began to fill with the interior of the Breachwinde's mess hall. He saw himself sitting across the room with Code Pink beside him.

"We're inside one of the guard's minds," Code Pink replied.

Avi was impressed by his friend's showcase of power. In the time they knew each other, Avi had never seen Apax do anything more than transmit thoughts. The pink PRO relied heavily on his discharger and sharp wits in combat.

"Does he know anything about where they're keeping Code Black?" Avi thought.

Code Pink appeared beside Avi in thought as they looked out through the guard's mental view. "Nothing that helps us," Apax stated, "I can't go too deep into his mind. Otherwise, this guard might feel me influencing his memories."

"Okay, well can you take over his mind?" Avi asked. Apax felt the yellow PRO's curiosity growing. "I'll possess one, you possess the other," Avi added.

"What would that accomplish?" Apax challenged, "We'd get ourselves killed before we even found Code Black, let alone made it off this ship."

"So what do we do now?" Avi thought. He stared at himself across from his vantage point in the guard's mind.

"I thought you wanted to be PROTO Yellow," Apax stated, "I don't have a plan. But if you come up with something that doesn't get us killed before we reach Promethean, I'm in."

CLAUDIUS COLONY
Dwarf Planet Estrella - Sunviza
Revan-V
Code Green

    Kiwa gripped the controls in her hands as she piloted the Revan-V over the metallic city. They dodged enemy artillery fire as the green Promethean focused on keeping the ship in the air. She had planned a kamikaze attack once before on the Emperor's palace but didn't need to execute it then. This time she figured if she couldn't save her ship she would use it to make an opening in the Sunrizas' castle.

    Kiwa's monitors lit up with an analysis of the damage the ship's hull had taken during the enemy onslaught. She had to act fast while the ship still had the means to send an SOS request to Code Pink and Yellow. It would take a while to reach them, and just as long for the two to come to rescue the others, but it was something. The green PRO flipped the switch to deactivate the display panel after her message was sent.

    Kiwa recalled what AP had told her about the Sunrizas' and their metallic world, the Sunviza. The silver PRO had traveled across the astral plane, as he had done for the Pontoppidan mission.

What was happening now was unlike what Kiwa's friend had described to her or their team. She knew there wasn't a chance the Revan-V would make it back to Promethean in its current condition. She questioned what would happen to AP and the others next as she sped toward the tower. One thing was certain, she wasn't going to leave her ship alone to die.

Smoke trailed from the Revan-V as it passed the city's edge flying over the pit under the floating castle. Kiwa braced herself in her seat as her fingers tightened around the steering wheel. She felt the ship rock up and down through the air as it swayed along its path.

Just a little further, she shared her thoughts with the Revan-V.

They focused on the Sunrizas' castle directly ahead as they examined a good point to make contact.

Before the Revan-V could reach its target they were pulled down into the pit below. Kiwa strained as she pulled up on the controls to no avail. The ship continued its descent through the pit; which was a tunnel connecting to the planet below. As they fell the walls lit up around them the closer they got to the charred, blackened earth under the Sunviza. The surface of Estrella had been cut away by the parasitic planet's connection. The tunnel that Kiwa was pulled into burrowed deep below the planet's crust and into the core.

"Kiwa," A male voice called out from behind her inside the ship. The green Promethean turned around expecting to see AP projecting into the cockpit.

"Brek?" Kiwa whispered. She was stunned to see the man she had loved standing in the middle of the room with her in his purple and black attire.

The former Code Black nodded. "You look good Code Green," He replied. He approached Kiwa who stood from her seat and jumped into his arms.

She felt a familiar energy in his embrace as if he had never left her. "How are you here?" She questioned. Kiwa's reflection gazed back at herself through Brek's visor as he looked down at her.

"I'm not," He responded, "You've never been able to let go of the pain of losing me, and you're too eager to see me again. Think about your dreams and the people you could help, and quit wastin' your time on me and live your life."

His words hurt but they were true. She had given up on her goals and taken every chance she could to join him in the afterlife. As she hugged the phantom from her past she closed her eyes and said her goodbyes.

When she opened her eyes she was back in her seat where she was left to wonder if that was all in her head. Either way, it didn't matter. All that mattered was finding a way for her and the Revan-V to escape their premature end in the planet's core.

Kiwa could feel the lifeforce being siphoned by the Sunviza through its connection. She suspected they didn't have much time before Estrella's core would be depleted and void.

The Revan-V drifted toward the planet's volcanic core guided by its gravitational pull. Kiwa thought about her vision of Brek. She hoped it was real and that Brek's ability to manipulate pain somehow imprinted his memory in her. The glow of the core was filling the Revan-V's displays limiting Kiwa's view. She used her arm to shield her eyes behind her visor as she stood to exit the cockpit. Despite her resolve to keep going, it appeared she was out of options.

Before she could make it to the cockpit doors she heard a thud behind her. For a second she thought the ship had collided with the core but that wouldn't make sense if she was still alive. The green Promethean turned back to see a massive bird-man had hit the windshield of the ship.

"Howdy," Garude shouted through the cracked windshield of the Revan-V, "This 'yer ship?"

XVII CLAUDIUS COLONY
Dwarf Planet Estrella - Sunviza
Revan-V
Code Green

AP fired his discharger into the smoke stacks rising up from the ground between him and his enemy. The Dilemen were scattered throughout the metallic city surrounding the PROs. They returned light-based attacks of their own that cut through the smoke toward AP and Code Red. The red Promethean had returned to his human form and was taking cover behind a column beside AP.

"Where's Code Black?" AP shouted. He could hardly hear himself over the noise of their dischargers and the cries of Dilemen on the other end.

"We separated," Code Red replied, "He's out there in the shadows!" The red Promethean used his free hand to point from his crouched position out toward the Dilemen.

Code Black flew across the ground in his shadowy form as he enjoyed the open space to move. The Sunviza was well-lit from the nearby star limiting Code Black's movements. Now that they were concealed below the structures of the city he could cut loose.

He approached three Dilemen on a balcony that had taken aim at Code Silver and Red. His bold shadow moved up the side of the wall and into the balcony with the mechanical men. Code Black stretched his arm up from the ground below a Dileman's leg and wrapped his hand around its calf. Before the unit knew what had happened Code Black had sunk the first Dileman into the deck, crushing its leg. He ripped the other leg out from under the Dileman who impulsively fired a light beam, striking his ally.

With the two Dileman incapacitated, Code Black turned his attention to the third. He slowly rose up out of the shadows reclaiming his human form for the first time since leaving Red's shadow.

There was a buzzing noise before a Discharger bolt slammed into the Dileman's head. The plasma bullet ricocheted past Code Black, who didn't have time to react to the attack. He looked over the balcony to see Code Red lowering his discharger after taking the shot.

"I had him!" Code Black popped off before he leaped down from the balcony. The PRO stuck the landing safely atop his own shadow and then joined the others.

AP was impressed by the two Prometheans accompanying him and felt relieved to have them at his side. He looked around the area while Red and Black bantered. Something had changed from what he had seen when he visited through the astral plane.

Code Yellow wasn't with them, and he was worried if she could survive alone against a sun god, or if any of them could. Whatever caused them to end up in their current position came with a greater risk to the Seven Colonies. AP wasn't sure how much time they would have to stop General Gold once they freed Code White and Blue. And without Kiwa and the Revan-V, they'd need a miracle to get off the planet in time to make a difference in the Colonies.

   There was a change in the air as they felt a static charge build-up around them. AP's head was on a swivel reflecting the swelling light of the fallen Dilemen in his silver visor. Their mechanical bodies floated and assembled into one magnetized beast. The tech creature continued to grow as it absorbed more parts into itself. Dozens of Dileman batteries circled the tank-like beast acting as a halo above its head.

   The juggernaut lifted its rebuilt arm into the air and aimed its palm at the three PROs. One of the battery cores launched from its position in the floating ring above the Dileman's head. AP and the others split up to avoid the battery that blew up on impact. The Dileman had outgrown the PROs who avoided the monster's stomps as it charged at Red and Black. AP watched the three fight while he looked for the discharger he'd dropped in the explosion.

Code Red shapeshifted into a clone of the Dileman, matching its large size. Code Black reinforced Red's shadow once more. The two began to gain the upper hand on the Dileman tank when Code Red suggested that AP go on without them.

AP was reluctant to go but it would give him the time he needed to find a way into the castle hovering above the city. He told the others to meet up with him once they were finished and then he parted ways with Code Red and Black. As he dashed off toward the center of the city he could hear the echoes of several explosions erupt behind him.

CLAUDIUS COLONY
Dwarf Planet Estrella
Planet Core
Code Green

Kiwa said goodbye to the Revan-V as her ship plunged into the core of the dwarf planet Estrella. She lost her connection to the ship's signal as she rode on the Werepheonix Garude's back. As the two flew along he explained who he was and how he came to be hiding in the core of the planet.

He told her about the first Sunriza to visit their world, who feasted on the native Uzalech. The truth was Garude had been eaten alive by the god but survived inside his stomach. There he consumed the sun god's flesh and drank from his veins. He managed to slowly kill the god from within, becoming a WerePheonix in the process.

"All this is happening because of you?" Kiwa asked. The Green PRO wasn't accusing him she was trying to understand the Sunriza's motives more. She adjusted her grip around Garude's long neck as he carried them through the air.

The WerePheonix hissed in response to Kiwa's question. "Yeah," He said, "You could say that." His massive wings flapped as he ascended through the tunnel bridging the two worlds. "You could also say I was fed-up with him takin' advantage of my people simply for living under his star," Garude added.

Kiwa still didn't blame Garude for standing up for his people knowing what she had learned. She wanted to know more about what he was doing in the planet's core though.

"You said you came down here to recover after the other two sun gods appeared?" Kiwa recalled.

Garude nodded.

"They killed our mounts, the toar, then captured as many of us as they could," The Uzalech sighed, "I couldn't save any of them. I couldn't risk giving back the power I stole from the previous Sunriza either so I ran."

Kiwa looked back at what was left of the burning core of the planet bubbling up below them. The hollow center of Estrella was crumbling around them, collapsing in on itself. "You came down here because they cut off your access to the star, so you found the next best source of energy," Kiwa added.

Garude laughed and said, "You catch on quick. I found my way down here but when the Sunviza began sucking the life from the planet I got stuck in this vacuum."

Kiwa turned her gaze from the core back to Garude. "What if we could disconnect the Sunviza and stop it from draining the planet's core?" She asked.

Garude glanced back at her over his shoulder and smirked. "We'd need a pretty big weapon to pull off somethin' like that," He replied, "You got anything that powerful on ya?"

"I think I could do it," Kiwa stated. She looked back at the core before she explained her ability to manipulate energy. "I have a plan, She added, "If I can overcharge the Sunviza's connection that should break the vacuum so we can escape. My friends are gonna need our help on the surface."

Garude smiled as he shifted in mid-air to fly back to the core with Kiwa in the hopes of saving what was left of his planet.

XVIII CLAUDIUS COLONY
Dwarf Planet Estrella - Sunviza
Code Silver

AP stood at the center of the city and stared down at the grains of metal that flowed toward the pit's magnetic pull. The Sunviza waterfalled into the pit below forming the connection to Estrella's core.

The Silver PRO took a deep breath and then glanced up at the floating castle towering above the clouds of ash. He reflected on his astral trip here before departing Promethean. He had already met with the Sunriza's Zol and Reya to make a deal for the others.

"Zol!" AP shouted to the heavens, "Why have you forsaken me?"

A chill ran down his spine in the silence that followed. He swallowed the lump in his throat as a sound of thunder echoed above.

The elder Sunriza's laughter shifted the atmosphere, producing lightning in the ashy sky. The crimson energy scattered through the swirling clouds forming around the castle above.

AP kept his composure as he spotted the Sunriza's silhouette slowly exit the castle. High above the Promethean, the Sunriza Zol levitated into the clouds. His body emitted a bluish glow in his muscular form draped in godly garb. The alien's long robes dangled past his feet as he descended through the air toward AP.

"You actually came," Zol said. The alien smirked as he stopped above the rim of the pit.

the silver Promethean trembled as he stared up at the Sunriza before him. AP's original plan was to avoid conflict on this mission. Lo had warned him against trying to combat the godlike alien's power.

"We had a deal," AP replied.

Zol's smirk turned into a scowl. "Your friends in exchange for the star and this planet?" Zol questioned. "We get nothing that was not already ours," The sun god added, "and your friend is still serving his sentence. I went light on him but the girl wasn't so lucky."

AP looked to the castle beyond the Sunriza. "Are you keeping them in there?" He asked, pointing to the structure floating behind Zol.

The Sunriza's smirk returned to his old, wrinkled alien face. "The last of the birds are being prepped as we speak. Plucked and seasoned to my liking," Zol laughed. "As for your friends," He added, "The girl is at the top of my castle. After our deal, I found out she could glimpse into my past so I had my Dilemen find a way to harness her power for me. 'Been around a long time, and even a god like myself forgets what he can do."

"What about Lo?" AP asked from the ground below.

"Who?" Zol replied, "Oh, right, he's the one in my ultralight prism, you'll join him soon enough."

Zol raised his hand as soon as his words left his lips and emitted a beam of light from his palm toward AP. The projectile attack came quickly but the silver PRO was able to sidestep it at the last second. He felt the same feeling he had felt earlier when Code Yellow altered his perception.

Must be a lingering effect, AP thought. He turned back to the sun god hovering above him.

a faint trail of smoke lingered from Zol's palm as his arm hung in the air. The Sunriza was impressed by AP's quick reflexes. Zol's fingers and hand tensed up as he fired another light-based attack.

AP rolled out of the way and drew his discharger to return fire on the Sunriza. He squeezed the trigger on the plasma weapon firing bolt after bolt at Zol above.

Instantly the Sunriza had teleported in front of AP to avoid the attack and close the gap on his opponent. The silver PRO jumped back startled as the towering sun god leapt toward him. Slamming his fist into the metal soil where AP had stood Zol scoffed as the human evaded him once more.

There was a rumbling below the ground at their feet that they mistook as an aftershock from Zol's attack. In actuality, it was the result of Kiwa's plan to disrupt the Sunviza's recharge via Estrella's core. The pit below the castle echoed the sonic boom made by Garude after he was able to escape the power vacuum with Kiwa.

AP and Zol, still unable to strike one another, faced off as the wind kicked up ash around them. The silver PRO checked the gauge on his discharger to see its plasma status. The weapon was at thirteen percent ammo capacity after the battle in the city earlier.

"Running out of juice already?" Zol laughed. He kept his distance from his position in the sky and began to orbit around AP taunting the PRO to attack.

Code Silver lowered his discharger and closed his eyes. He focused on his surroundings and recreated them inside the astral plane in his mind. AP watched Zol's pattern for a chance to strike and anticipated the outcome of each way he could attack. When he was ready he opened his eyes and made his move.

The silver PRO fired his discharger in Zol's direction but the Sunriza sped up to dodge the shot.

"You're boring me," Zol confessed.

The Sunriza heard a noise above him and looked up to see AP falling from the clouds toward him. Zol dodged the heel of the silver PRO's flying kick and swung his glowing arm out to catch his falling assailant. The projection of AP dissolved into ash as Zol realized he had been deceived by the human. He turned his head with lightning speed to see the silver PRO hurdling up toward him with his fist extended.

AP's punch landed the first blow as he felt his bones fracture in his left hand against the Sunriza's nose. The sun god spun backward through the air as he clung to his face. AP freefalled down to the edge of the pit landing on his chest, breaking bones and knocking the wind out of him.

Zol regained his composure and stopped himself in midair. He swung his arms away from his bloodied nose in anger and split the winds in two directions. The break in the ash-laced clouds caused the star above to shine down on them once more. Zol looked up and drank its radiation, healing himself.

AP propped himself up on his elbows as he heard the boom of thunder once more, only this time it was the return of Reya. The young Sunriza lit up the sky as she regrouped with Zol in the clouds above the pit. AP noticed Reya was carrying the body of Code Yellow by the collar of her Promethean armor.

"Have you changed your mind about helping me?" Zol scoffed, "Took you long enough."

Reya glanced down at Code Silver on the ground below then back at her elder Sunriza. "No!" Reya barked back, "We came to get revenge on the Werephoenix for killing our kin and we got that. I'll not extinguish my only star for a memory that some human showed you." She tossed Code Yellow's unconscious body to the ground near AP.

Zol growled as he watched a figure emerge from the outskirts of the city. It was the Dileman tank Code Red and Black had stayed behind to fight. He turned his attention back to Reya in the air with him as the techno figure continued its approach on the ground.

"Ordinarily I would agree with you child, but this is no memory, this is expansion," Zol replied. "We'll prune your star out of this sky and take it somewhere it can truly blossom," Zol added.

Reya shook her head as her body swelled with more light from within her. "I said no!" She argued, "There's too much life in this system that depends on this star to take it anywhere else."

Zol laughed and said, "We'll attract greater lifeforms beyond the scope of this system. It'll thrive, we'll take it and hide it in Crude Space, we both know they could use a star out there."

AP listened to the two Sunrizas go back and forth while he tried to understand what they were talking about. He noticed something approaching from within the pit below the sun gods. The tank that had defeated Code Red and Code Black stood guard over AP and Yellow on the ground as it awaited a command.

Zol and Reya's conversation was cut short by Kiwa and Garude as the pair shot up out of the mouth of the pit. The two flew between the Sunrizas with the Green PRO jumping from Garude's back to strike Zol in the face. After the attack, Kiwa latched onto the sun god to siphon his energy using her ability. Zol's energy pool was enormous and backfired on Kiwa, flinging the Green PRO from the sun god in the sky.

Reya was closing the gap flying after Garude when the Dileman tank on the ground turned on her. The massive techno figure had been Code Red in disguise who continued to open fire on the Sunriza Reya. She grew irritated with the humans as she dodged their attack from the ground and returned a palm blast of her own. The Sunriza's attack engulfed the Dileman tank in light, leaving only a shadow on the ground below.

Reya stopped in the air to observe the repercussions of her actions. She thought it was a Dileman acting on Zol's behalf but she felt a human presence extinguish in her light.

AP looked over from his position on the ground to see where his teammates had once stood. He could hear a faint voice calling out from the shadow of the blast that remained and crawled to it.

"Code Black?" AP called out as he dragged his beaten body across the metal scrap of the Sunviza's surface. He reached the edge of the charred shadow from the silhouette of the Dileman tank where Code Red had stood.

"Ye-yeah, I'm in here," Code Black coughed and confessed, "I'm not ready to go, but I can't get up either."

AP reached out and placed his hand on the shadow left behind and asked, "Is there anything I can do to help you?"

Code Black coughed again and said, "Don't leave me here. If I could stand up I would, But maybe," He coughed again, "Maybe I could be your shadow for a while?"

AP looked at the ground and nodded and asked, "What do I need to do?"

Code Black pulled AP's hand into the ground burying his fingertips into the soil. "Remember me," Code Black said in a whisper, "Don't forget about your pal Endy, who carried you to the Silver Sanction."

AP nodded as he felt his shadow become heavy with the weight of his friend, giving him strength. The silver Promethean rose up from the ground recovered from his fall earlier.

"You're Code Silver in my eyes, Endy," AP said. There was no response as he looked up to the battle raging above in the sky.

Kiwa was riding Garude's back once again through the air as they swerved between the two Sunrizas. Reya clashed with her elder sun god Zol as she avoided his attacks as well. The Werephoenix Garude was on the offensive as he spat orange flames from his mouth at the evasive gods.

They're all going at it, AP thought to himself, *maybe I have a chance to get to Lo and Ciela in Zol's castle.* He focused on the floating tower lingering in the clouds above the ash and looked for an entry point. The cylindrical structure had no windows or doors that AP could see so his only course of action was to aim for the top. He closed his eyes and focused on projecting to the top and what the air would feel like up there. In an instant, he felt it on his body as he left the surface of the Sunriza through the astral plane. He felt himself motioning to the top of the castle where he now stood.

The silver PRO looked back over the balcony ledge to see Zol flying straight up at him. AP jumped back to avoid the Sunriza as Garude tailed close behind him. Kiwa jumped from Garude's back to be with AP on the castle deck. The two quickly embraced when they saw each other again as a gust of wind brought Reya face to face with them.

"Where do you think you're going?" Reya shouted. She lunged toward the two Prometheans on top of the castle but she was stopped in her tracks by Zol. The elder caught Reya by her long white hair and hissed, "I could ask the same of you, now harvest that star in the sky for us."

Zol pulled Reya back by her hair and lifted her alien body toward the star shining above them as she screamed.

"I won't do it!" Reya shouted.

The elder Sunriza scoffed then lifted Reya and grabbed her leg with his free hand, ripping her in half at the waist. AP and Kiwa watched helplessly as Reya cried out. Roots from inside her body rained down spores of stardust over Zol as he began to glow brighter than before. His appearance changed as he took on a slim form, sprouting bulbs along his shoulders, arms, and back.

Zol tossed Reya to the side as the roots protruding from her two halves began to entangle themselves. The remaining sun god turned back to AP and Kiwa and laughed. "She'll live," Zol said, "Can't say the same about the rest of you."

The Sunriza levitated into the air as he stared down at AP. "I've enjoyed our battle together," Zol stated, "You shall will live on in my memory as the Battle of Ash and Stars." The Sunriza paused then added, "Until I forget you in a few centuries. Now if you'll excuse me, Prometheans, I'm taking my star and going home."

Zol rotated in the air to turn his back on AP and Kiwa then rocketed into the sky toward the stars. Garude tried to fly after him but it was no use, Zol had gone outside the Sunviza's atmosphere.

Above his alien tech world, the Sunriza began to speak to the star in his long-forgotten language. His words echoed as Zol spoke the prayer from his memories, putting his blessing on the star. When he was done claiming the star he lifted his hands and the Sunviza below him began to part. The alien world previously encased Estrella but now it shifted to form a conelike dish aimed at the star. The shift in gravity from the Sunviza catipulted the near hollow dwarf Estrella out of its orbit. The planets charred surface crumbled away surrounding the lost planet with debris.

Zol began blossoming flowers on his body to accelerate his photosynthesis process. When he was finished he stood in the center of his creation and began to siphon the light out of the sky and into himself.

XIX CLAUDIUS COLONY
Dwarf Planet Estrella - Sunviza
Code Silver and Green

    AP and Kiwa watched as Zol continued to drain the star out of the sky above them. Garude returned to the Sunriza's castle carrying the unconscious yellow Promethean from below.
    "What now?" Garude asked. His raven feathers stood up when he saw Reya's body lying in the corner reattaching its two halves. "And why is she still alive?" He added.
    AP and Kiwa looked at the fallen Sunriza nearby and then back at Garude who was still holding Code Yellow.
    "Let's figure out a way to get inside this castle," AP said, turning to Reya and emphasizing, "All of us."
    Kiwa glanced at the platform they stood on and looked for any cracks or entry points but found none. "It's sealed off," The green Promethean stated, "But if we can get inside I might be able to fly it off-world."
    "Are you sure you can do it?" AP asked.
    "Course she can," Garude interrupted, "You shoulda seen her part the planets, She ripped the Sunviza a new one!"

AP turned to Code Green. "Is that true?" He asked.

Kiwa nodded and said, "There's more I have to tell you, but right now we have to focus on getting inside. If this castle levitates it should be operational."

"You'll never get in," Reya called out. Her voice was weak and dry.

AP and Kiwa turned to check on the sun god. Reya's body was reattached but she still had roots dangling from her wounds.

"Can you help us?" AP asked. He knelt down and offered his right hand to Reya. The Sunriza was reluctant at first but then took the human's hand.

"Only because I heard what you said, about all of us making it out of here, Promethean," Reya replied, "Follow me." The young Sunriza limped to the center of the platform as Zol drained the last bit of light from the star in the sky.

Reya activated the castle causing the center of the platform to open up. The opening's circumference expanded to allow the group to enter. The sky above fell into darkness as Zol engulfed the full power of the star.

"Get inside!" AP shouted. The silver PRO looked up to the heavens as he waited for the others to enter the castle. His eyes locked with Zol's godlike alien gaze sending chills through his body.

The elder Sunriza teleported down and swooped AP up by his silver sash and carried him into the sky.

"AP!" Kiwa called out. She was the last person on the platform as she watched her friend get dragged away.

"Kiwa, get inside, please," Garude insisted.

The green Promethean climbed into the alien castle before Reya sealed the opening. She looked around at the strange tech inside and the few remaining Dileman that operated it all.

"Do you need me?" Kiwa commented. She pointed out the guards to Reya and Garude.

"Yes," Reya said, "They don't know the first thing about flying."

The Sunriza led Kiwa and Garude through the castle and into the main chambers. Garude put Code Yellow down on a table while Reya led Kiwa to Code Blue.

"Zol experimented on her," Reya warned, "She's different now."

"Let me see her," Kiwa stated.

Reya nodded and waved her hand over a wall activating an opening. Kiwa stepped inside as Reya followed after her. In the center of the room was a round glass bulb. The bulb was projecting flashes of the Sunriza Zol's life on its surface. Inside, Kiwa found Code Blue, Ciela, attached to alien tech. The blue PROs arms and legs had been amputated and had wiring protruding from the limbs. Her helmet was removed and her head shaved, with the back of her head replaced by more tech.

"Oh my," Kiwa said. She couldn't believe that was her former teammate. She placed her hand on the glass. The connection woke Ciela inside. The blue PRO's eyes shot open and then shed a tear upon seeing her former teammate.

"With the right technology you'll be able to extract her," Reya commented, "It's the other one we have to worry about."

Kiwa said goodbye to Ciela and then went with Reya to another floor of the castle. There they found a prism of light where Lo's spirit was encased.

"You can't get him out?" Kiwa asked.

Reya shook her head.

"He's in another dimension now. It was pointless for you to come here," Reya confessed, "Zol saw an opportunity to trick the Silver one into coming."

"AP?" Kiwa asked, "But why him?"

Reya shrugged. "He came to him in one of Zol's visions. Something about him reminded my elder of another he battled long ago," Reya remarked.

XX CLAUDIUS COLONY
Dwarf Planet Estrella - Sunviza
Code Silver

Zol dragged AP through the ashy clouds as crimson lightning crackled around them. The alien held him with one hand and threw a series of punches at the human with his free fist. Each blow echoed with thunderous rumbles as AP took the pummeling from the god.

"You're nothing like I hoped you would be, Promethean," Zol commented. He stopped his barrage to hold AP at eye level.

"I don't know what you're talking about," AP groaned. He grabbed onto the Sunriza's forearm with his hands and tried to get free.

Zol flung a fist into AP's gut, breaking the human's grip on his arm.

"Well then I have no reason left to keep you around," Zol mocked, "Step into the light, I'm sure you see it by now."

The Sunriza unleashed a flurry of lazers on AP from the flowers along his body. The final light beam swatted the silver Promethean down to the planets coned surface. AP landed with a thud in the metal soil but it still wasn't enough to knock him out for good.

He struggled to get to his feet as his knees buckled under his weight, but he felt Endy's presence backing him.

Zol smirked, impressed by the human's resilience.

"As I suspected, human, you walk with a light of your own," Zol said, "Allow me to bring that light out of you!"

He raised his palm and produced an orb of light that grew larger than his alien body and released it toward AP.

The silver Promethean braced himself and thought about his brother for whom he was doing all of this for.

As the orb grew closer AP's vision faded to white. He prepared to meet his end when a mysterious figure teleported in front of him. AP held his hand over his visor to block the light and get a better view.

The person wore unfamiliar Promethean armor, including a bronze helmet with two horns. The mysterious bronze figure gave AP a thumbs up before absorbing the full force of the light attack. The impact resulted in an explosion of ash and dust that kicked up into the air. When the smoke settled AP saw the new Promethean, Code Bronze, unscathed.

Zol's surprise turned to anger and his flowers fired a cluster of light orbs at the Bronze warrior.

Code Bronze flew into the air and absorbed the impact of each shot, going out of the way at times to do so.

Zol watched Code Bronze fly at him with incredible speed as he prepared another attack. Bronze teleported behind Zol before he could react and elbowed the alien in the back of the neck. The horned PRO followed up by launching a series of light orbs back at the Sunriza.

The PRO released the stored light from Zol back on him and then charged in for a physical assault against the god. Code Bronze finished by sending an uppercut into Zol's abdomen. The PRO hit Zol with enough strength it caused the aliens back to split and unravel his roots.

Zol hovered backwards from Code Bronze as he began to cough up starspores. AP watched from the ground as the Sunriza vomited a glowing seed larger than all of them.

Code Bronze reached out and claimed the seed from Zol, who withered and fell from the sky defeated.

AP watched Zol crash into the Sunviza like a meteor. The silver PRO turned his attention to Code Bronze in the sky after Zol's impact.

Code Bronze didn't say a word but gave AP an affirming nod before teleporting away with the seed.

CLAUDIUS COLONY
Sunriza's Castle
Code Silver and Green

Thanks to Garude, AP regrouped with the others at the Sunriza's castle. He was relieved to be back with the surviving members of his team and ready to leave the system.

"What happened out there?" Reya asked, "Where is Zol?"

AP was hurt and in Kiwa's embrace but he managed to point down to the planet below.

"Something strange happened, Zol threw up a seed and wilted away," AP remarked.

"Did you defeat him?" Kiwa asked. She was happy to be reunited with her friend and hesitant to let go of him just yet.

AP shook his head.

"Zol doesn't matter, where is the seed?" Reya asked. Her voice was shaky and audibly concerned.

AP shook his head again.

"Someone showed up and saved me out of the blue," AP confessed, "Whoever it was took the seed with them."

Reya scoffed and stepped up to AP grabbing him by his sash. "You didn't save my star seedling?" She shouted. The Sunriza pushed AP back as she released her grip. "You might as well have given it to Zol," She added under her breath.

    AP shrugged and apologized. "I didn't know," He said.

    Reya scoffed and then turned her back on the Prometheans.

    "Leave now," Reya said, "Take this castle and those disgusting Uzalech and leave this world. The remaining Dileman will assist you on your journey."

    "What about you?" AP asked.

    Reya shook her head. "I have nothing left without my star," She confessed, "I wish to be alone here with Zol."

    AP and the others thanked the young Sunriza before she left the castle. After Reya was gone AP turned to Kiwa and asked about Lo and Ciela. She took him to see their allies and reason for traveling to Estrella.

    When they reached Code White in his prism AP placed his palm on the glowing construct. He concentrated on Lo inside, and began to enter and exit the astral plane on opposite sides of the prism.

Code White sat up inside his dimensional prison as AP created a rift within the astral plane to the real world. The white Promethean stepped up to AP and grabbed his astral shoulder and used his own ability to phase out.

Back in the real world, AP took Lo to see Ciela as Garude and Kiwa took command of the castle and set off for Promethean.

XXI AUGUSTUS COLONY
Promethean
Code Silver

Kiwa piloted the alien craft into the orbit of the Promethean homeworld. She lowered the castle down over the library where it hovered in its idle state. Garude and AP commanded the Dilemen to free the Uzalech and Toar kept in the lower chambers. The Werephoenix was relieved to see his cousin Senk unharmed along with his wife and kids. AP regretted his initial deal to leave the Uzalech in Zol's possession once he saw them. He offered the birdlike people a place to stay on Promethean until they found a more permanent home.

The local Prometheans all gathered along the library steps to see Code Silver return. AP checked on Lo and Ciela in her chamber before he exited the castle. Lo had not left Code Blue's side since he escaped the Sunriza's prism. AP sent word for the medical teams to extract the injured inside the castle.

The medics stabilized the comatose blue PRO and removed her from the glass bulb she was encased in. Lo and AP left with them on the floating platform that descended down from the castle. The crowd below had a mixed reception to AP's return. There were cheers while others protested AP's claim to the title and the results of his sanction.

AP parted ways with Lo and the others who left on their way to the medical facilities. The silver PRO caught up with Kiwa who had reunited with Apax and Avi, Code Pink and Yellow respectively.

The four PROs shared their excitement to be together again on their homeworld. AP looked around for the new Code Black that his friends had retrieved.

"Where is he?" AP asked.

Apax and Avi glanced at each other and then back at Code Silver.

"You're not gonna like this," Apax replied, "He's with Topaz Jack. They're here on Promethean in General Gold's tower."

"Why is Topaz Jack here?" AP questioned.

"They captured us before we left the Port of Pius," Avi confessed. He looked over at Code Pink beside him and added, "I thought about what'd be best for all of us, and decided to surrender. Sure enough, Jack let us go once we got here."

AP nodded and agreed with Code Yellow's decision. "I would have done the same," AP stated.

Code Silver wasted no time heading to the General's tower with his unit close behind. The silver PRO opened the tall golden doors at the base of the tower and found Topaz Jack sitting at the end of the room. A slim Code Black was standing beside him along with his Topaz guards.

"Jack!" AP shouted, "What brings you to Promethean?" The silver PRO looked over at Code Black who started to move toward him. AP motioned for Code Black to stop who obeyed his command.

"You should be thanking me," Topaz Jack laughed. He pointed to Code Black and said, "He'd be dead if it weren't for me. did you think I didn't know what was going on?"

"What's he talking about?" Kiwa asked. She was standing behind AP along with Apax and Avi.

"He didn't tell you?" Topaz Jack laughed, "That's rich. Your buddy here thought he could stick his nose in the Emperor's business. Ya see, he sent you on a suicide mission for this kid." Topaz Jack pointed over to Code Black as he spoke.

"I can explain," AP said, turning to his team. "Everything I've done has been for my brother," the Silver Promethean confessed.

Kiwa stepped toward AP and placed a hand on his shoulder. "We know, AP, to avenge Brek," Kiwa said.

AP looked down and then back at Code Black behind him and sighed. "I avenged Brek when I proved Elma was behind his murder. Everything else has been to protect my other brother. My half-brother."

AP kept his focus on Code Black. "It's an honor to introduce everyone to my brother, Marcus. Son of Emperor Zemula, and rightful heir," AP declared.

Topaz Jack stood from his seat and approached the others gathered around Marcus and AP. He turned toward AP and released a cloud of vapor from his helmet's vents. "There's something else you need to know," Jack said, "About the General."

AP and the other's looked around. He was surprised he hadn't realized General Gold wasn't in his own tower.

"What about him?" AP asked.

Topaz Jack Sighed. "He knows the truth about you," Jack confessed, "That your allegiances lie with the Aurelians. The General made the first move while you were distracted."

"What's he talking about, AP?" Kiwa asked, "Topaz Jack, what did the General do?"

"Hyper-Train," Code Black blurted out. The young Promethean caught the others off guard with his outburst. Marcus rubbed his arm nervously as he repeated himself while AP tried to calm him down.

"The kid's never wrong," Topaz Jack said. He waited for Marcus' nervous tick to pass before he continued. "He'd be a goner if it weren't for me," Jack stated, "you see, after I picked them up the General attacked the Hyper-Train."

"You're kidding!" Avi shouted out. He looked at Apax beside him who nodded to confirm the news from reading Jack's mind.

Topaz Jack turned to the PROs and stated, "I don't like jokes."

Jack continued, "I wish I were making this up. Shortly after leaving the Port of Pius every car on the Hyper-Train imploded, they're gone."

AP thought about all the innocent lives aboard the Hyper-Train killed by General Gold. "Emperor Yujen is behind this," AP stated, "He ordered the General to attack Aurelius to lure out my brother. Gold must've found out Marcus was going to be on the Hyper-Train."

"I don't think so," Topaz Jack replied, "I've got eyes and ears everywhere. My Rejects reported the General's ship entering the Aurelius Colony after the bombing. He's still looking for your brother."

"Why would he attack the Hyper-Train if he didn't know about this guy?" Apax asked. He tried reading Topaz Jack's mind for the answers but felt himself blocked this time.

"My guess," Topaz Jack said, "General Gold wanted to frame the Aurelians. Word is already spreading within the other colonies that they were behind the attack."

AP looked to the others as he formed a plan. "Kiwa, do you think you can get us to Aurelius?" He asked.

The green Promethean froze.

"Unfortunately, that's not going to be possible," Topaz Jack interrupted.

AP turned to the Reject confused by his statement. "And why wouldn't we?" The silver PRO replied, "I'm second in command here."

Topaz Jack exhaled another burst of vapor from his helmet. "Because," Topaz Jack declared, "It wouldn't do any good. The Aurelians have a secret trump card waiting for Gold. And Mama Topaz knows with the General out of the way, I'm taking over this operation."

AP and the others paused before breaking out into laughter.

"Don't laugh at your new General," Topaz Jack shouted. He cocked his head back as he mused over the title of General Topaz.

"Why would I let you claim the Prometheans as your own?" AP asked.

"What choice do you have?" Topaz Jack asked, "Do you think you'd be a better fit to fill the General's shoes? You're good at getting Prometheans killed just like Gold was, I'll give ya that much."

AP thought about how many of his teammates had fallen in the short time he had been a Promethean. He reflected on Endy and Code Red's losses during the Battle of Ash and Stars. He recalled the unit lost in the Emperor's palace, where he should have died. Then he remembered something General Gold had told the Emperor afterward. Gold had mentioned that AP was the key to Pontopiddan, and they were connected. He had a trump card of his own this entire time.

"It's true I'm no leader," AP began, "We'll manage to get by without you, Jack. See, I have something neither you nor the General could wield, I have the moon." The silver Promethean raised his hand above his head as he pointed to the sky. High above the manmade world of the Prometheans, Pontoppidan slumbered.

Topaz Jack stared into AP's visor from across the room. "You don't know what you're doing," Topaz Jack laughed, "You can't control that Abysmal moon."

AP lowered his hand from above his head and clenched his fist, then smirked underneath his helmet.

"Awaken," AP shouted, "Pontoppidan!"

High above the planet the Abysmal moon heard AP's cry and was lulled from his sleep. The alien creature stretched its long tentacles filling the skies above Promethean.

Topaz Jack heard the roar of the Abysmal moon from inside General Gold's tower. The aliens cry sent chills down Jack's spine causing his knees to tremble. He swallowed the lump in his throat and regained his composure.

"Very well," Jack stated, "But don't expect me to help you again after this, Reject. It's going to be hard to protect him on your own." He turned and shot a smoky glance at Code Black, then ordered his Topaz guards to follow him out of the tower.

AUGUSTUS COLONY
Promethean
Code Green

    AP and the others wasted no time preparing for their journey to Aurelius after Topaz Jack left. Kiwa was relieved to see her friend AP happy to be reunited with his brother Marcus. She couldn't believe that after all this time, Brek and AP had kept Marcus a secret from her. She found comfort in knowing that her friend was back with his family.

    Avi and Apax were eager to get out and help AP however they could after missing the battle of ash and stars. The two Prometheans parted ways with AP and Marcus in order to rally more PROs to join them on their next mission.

    Kiwa was finally alone with her friend as he made his final preparations.

    "AP," Kiwa called out. Her friend was seated where Topaz Jack had been at the General's desk inside his tower.

    "What is it?" AP called out. The silver PRO didn't look up from the galactic map spread out before him.

    Kiwa stepped up to the desk and took a seat across from AP.

"It's about the next mission," Kiwa began, "I don't think I can go with you."

AP looked up from the galactic map and sighed. "Why not?" He asked, before adding, "I can't save my colony alone."

Kiwa looked across the room at Marcus who was meditating nearby.

"You won't be alone," Kiwa replied, "You two have each other now, and there's something else out there for me. Away from the Prometheans." She was hesitant to say the last part aloud.

"What do you mean?" AP questioned.

Kiwa sighed and looked down at the galactic map before returning her gaze to AP.

"I'm tired," Kiwa said, "After I lost Brek I desperately wanted to be with him again. During the battle back on Estrella, right before the Revan-V went down, I saw him. I saw Brek."

AP was surprised to hear this revelation. He thought about the mysterious Code Bronze, and began to wonder who really saved them.

"What did he say to you?" AP asked.

"He reminded me of a greater purpose," Kiwa said, "Before I lost Brek I dreamed of becoming a WorldPilot. I think it's time for me to chase that dream again."

AP sighed. "You're sure this is what you want?" He replied.

Kiwa nodded.

"Okay," AP remarked, "Code Green, I hearby relinquish you from your duty. You're free to leave the Promethans and follow your dreams."

Kiwa's smile was concealed by her green helmet as she thanked AP.

She got up and hugged him, feeling guilty for leaving, but she knew they would see each other again.

As she stepped into the sunlight outside General Gold's tower she felt free. Their was a familiar figure waiting for her near the entrance.

Garude the Werephoenix, leaned against the wall as his head cocked up. "Where ya goin'?" He asked.

Kiwa stared back at her new friend and said, "I don't know yet."

Garude looked around the manmade world where his people were settling in and smiled.

"Mind if I come with you?"

End of Crude Space
Part III

Milton Keynes UK
Ingram Content Group UK Ltd.
UKHW040235031224
451863UK00001B/70